GAIA
& THE
MYSTERY
OF
KUKULKAN

ANIKO BRANG &NANCY SAROS

BEAVER'S
POND
PRESS

GAIA
& THE
MYSTERY
OF
KUKULKAN

Edited by Courtney Bain
Cover illustration by Vanessa Kuiper
Cover and interior design by Jay Monroe.

ISBN: 978-1-64343-631-9
Library of Congress Number: 2023904475
Printed in the United States of America
First Edition: 2023

27 26 25 24 23   5 4 3 2 1

Beaver's Pond Press
939 West Seventh Street
Saint Paul, MN 55102
(952) 829-8818
www.BeaversPondPress.com

BEAVER'S
POND
PRESS

To order, or to contact the authors, visit
www.AnikoBrangNancySaros.com.

Nancy Saros dedicates this book to her children and grandchildren. May you always hold dear a curious spirit.

Aniko Brang dedicates this book to her husband, Tim, for all his encouragement and support.

PROLOGUE

4.5 BILLION YEARS AGO...

The full moon's light illuminated the barren landscape of planet Earth. Multiple shades of brown extended endlessly among the sand and rock formations. One structure towered above all the rest. It was a tall, narrow pile of granite that seemed to extend to the heavens. Each rock appeared to have been strategically placed, although Earth was uninhabited by any living being at the time.

A rush of frigid air broke the stillness of the warm night air, stirring the dust and debris from where it had lain dormant for eons. Suddenly the air became thick with a haze as the forceful wind gained momentum with each passing second. Within a minute, land could not be differentiated from sky as a huge meteorite barreled down from the heavens. An intense blinding light lit up the entire sky and a deafening explosion shook the core of the Earth as this alien space object plummeted into the ground. Tiny remnants of the meteorite disintegrated into a fine dust on impact. The entire landscape had been shifted by the immense, newly created crater, except for one thing: the towering rock formation. The slender granite structure remained completely intact, its presence even more dominating than before. It was as if the formation not only extended upward but also into the bowels of the Earth. Its size seemed to have doubled with the newly formed crater.

The debris in the air thickened as it ascended quickly toward the moon. The sky grew a deeper, darker shade of brown. Millions of small remnants from the meteorite scattered on the floor of the crater. Some of the pieces began shifting back and forth. Tiny green specks wiggled out of the shattered meteorite as the dirty air closed its black curtain on planet Earth . . .

CHAPTER 1

BACK OF THE CLASS

Gaia sat coiled before her creative writing class waiting to present the plot of her latest story.

"All right, Gaia, let's hear your idea," prompted Miss Hissy from the back of the cave.

Miss Hissy drove Gaia crazy. She was always instructing her to say this, not that; don't slouch; always keep your scales shiny; don't question so much . . . blah, blah, blah.

Gaia adjusted her uniquely patterned coil, which consisted of three light stripes running the length of her short, olive-green, garter snake body. While the other garters in her class also had three stripes, they were all one color. Gaia had one white, one yellow, and between them, one shimmering light blue. Her beautiful skin seemed something only a great artist could have created, an artist her mother said lived in the heavens and was called Serpens. She stretched her body up as high as possible, her head now well above her classmates' bored, teenage faces. She tried to ignore the nervousness she felt rising within her, but then her nose began twitching.

She tried to focus on her hope that today might be the day Miss Hissy would just let her finish what she had to say without constant interruptions and advice. Gaia just wanted to say how she felt and be able to ask questions without getting into trouble all the time. But Miss Hissy did not allow curiosity to intrude into her classroom. Her school was well known for strict discipline and dogmatic adherence to the dictates of Moon Meadow's Grand Wizard, Mandihar. His *Guidance Manual for Young Snake Minds* was a sacred text to Miss Hissy, and she adhered to it absolutely.

Gaia cleared her throat as she tried to choose her words. She had to project her voice, being somewhat soft-spoken by nature; her parents had taught her not to be boisterous and loud. She wanted to be concise yet interesting. Looking out at the sea of classmates' expressionless faces made this a difficult feat.

"Come on Gaia, stop stalling. Scales up."

Gaia faked a smile. "Yes, Miss Hissy. My story is about a young girl snake."

Miss Hissy immediately cut Gaia off. She had spoken only a few measly words and already Miss Hissy was instructing her.

"We need details, Gaia. Who is this snake and where is she from? Details, Gaia. You must keep the reader engaged."

Gaia did all she could to keep from screaming and slithering out of the school cave and heading home. Her nose twitching increased. A wave of self-consciousness overwhelmed her, as she was certain all her classmates saw was a huge, spasming nose. She tried to be inconspicuous as she adjusted her head, pointing her nose upward.

"Yes, Miss Hissy. The snake is me, Gaia Coiler. I am thirteen years old and live in Moon Meadow with my family. Lucima is my best friend."

"Stop right there, Gaia."

Gaia felt defeated at not being able to continue. Her plot was a good one; she had given herself an alter ego, a female superhero-Moon Maiden, who possessed the special power of teleportation. But she didn't even have a chance to get that part out.

"What did I teach you about introductions?"

Gaia started to answer, her sad brown eyes staring at the ceiling.

"Look at me when speaking."

Gaia wanted to scream. Miss Hissy was unbearable.

"You said to make the intro compelling, edgy, different . . . to keep the reader engaged."

"Exactly, Gaia. Do you think what you have said so far is captivating?"

She shook her head no, feeling too humiliated in front of her peers to answer out loud. Her nose-twitching was now out of control.

"No, it is not, Gaia. In fact, it is quite dull. Come back to your mat and we will try again tomorrow."

Suddenly, all the other young snakes came alive and snickered, pointing the ends of their tails to their nose as Gaia slowly slithered back to her mat, now trying to keep her head pointed at the floor. All of them snickered except for Lucima and a new boy in the class named Kimba. Gaia really didn't know him yet but thought he was cute with his huge yellow eyes. He smiled at her as she slithered down the aisle to her mat. Miss Hissy called his name.

"Kimba, you are next."

Kimba headed to the front of the class. His slither had swagger, which intrigued Gaia. After the presentations, Miss Hissy returned to the front of the class. She always looked meticulously put together. Her lime-green scales sparkled in the sunlight, not a speck of dirt to be found. She tried to appear young, but Gaia could tell age was creeping up on Miss Hissy. Upon closer scrutiny, her perfectly polished scales were fading in color. Even though she tried hiding it, Gaia could see her slither had slowed and become stiffer than the younger snakes' movements. Gaia had to suppress her laughter as she came up with a nickname for her teacher, "Meticulous Hiss." She couldn't wait to tell Lucima.

Miss Hissy instructed the class that it was now story time, and the story today would be a myth, so there would be no need for questions afterward. She prefaced every story with the same introduction, which Gaia found weird. It was, however, in compliance with the part of Mandihar's *Guidance Manual for Young Snake Minds*, chapter 1, verse 13, which dealt with suppressing curiosity.

All the small garters rearranged themselves in a circle around Miss Hissy, eager to hear today's tale. Gaia loved story time; it was her favorite part of the school day. She crept over to Lucima and coiled up next to her.

Gaia and Lucima were soul mates, but they were a study in physical contrast. Lucima was about the same size as Gaia but lacked stripes, which was unusual, and her brownish-green skin was covered in lighter-green spots. Her huge round pupils were set in dark-brown eyes. One trait they shared was a humorous sense of the absurd. Together they settled in for story time, giving each other a knowing look as Miss Hissy fussed to adjust her coil perfectly.

CHAPTER 2

MOON MEADOW'S LEADER

Mandihar sat perched on his rock ledge high in the beautiful Atum Mountains that surrounded Moon Meadow. The setting sun's reflection bounced off the red stone embedded in his hood, casting a bright-crimson glow. Every night, he watched the small garter community hurrying home before the sky went dark. He smiled with satisfaction at how all the snakes obeyed his curfew without question, simply because he demanded it. He looked on as another busy day was coming to an end.

Small snake dens lined narrow, zigzagging dirt paths that ran through a large area of reed grasses, tall and broad-leafed with feathery white flower clusters. The garters' rock homes alternated between shades of brown and grey with the occasional dark-red stone. All had a medium-size entry shaft facing the path, but only some had the desired small window. The snakes took great pride in their residences and could be seen sweeping the entryways with their tails before turning in for the night.

It was a small community that was growing quickly, with many new homes popping up along the paths. One of the most sought-after jobs was in construction. Another popular occupation was farming at one of the rodent or frog farms.

Today was payday in Moon Meadow. Hundreds of snakes slithered down the paths toward home after a long day of work. Using their tails, they dragged behind them small bags woven from the stiff stems of dried reeds and filled with heavy loads of small pebbles, which markedly slowed down their slither. Mandihar noticed one of the rodent-farm workers seemed to be growing extra padding on his belly. He took out his carving stick and scratched the resident's name on the rock slab next to him. Mandihar scanned the names already etched in, noting the list was getting quite lengthy.

All the snakes eagerly rushed home with their earnings, which consisted of different-colored pebbles known as "mambas." They were simple, everyday small rocks found along the riverbank where Mandihar's crew collected them and hauled them up the long, winding trail to his expansive den. It was there that Mandihar oversaw many workers who used his special dyes to color the small rocks according to their monetary values.

Mandihar glanced off to the side at his garden of roses, marigolds, and indigo. One of the garter gardeners nodded a hello before quickly returning to work. Mandihar smiled at the sight of the flourishing flowers used for his secret mamba dye. He prohibited anyone else from growing these plants in

Moon Meadow and had his patrol guards check every garden nightly. On occasion, a defiant snake would be seen being dragged through the meadow up to Mandihar's den, sometimes to never be seen again. How he relished those nights. Two yellow-tinged fangs emerged as his smile widened at the thought. However, tonight looked quiet.

"Good little snakes," he thought to himself with slight disappointment.

He couldn't contain a small burst of laughter at the thought of the garters' hopes of wealth. His laughter grew a little louder as he thought of their unattainable dream.

"Don't tell them that," he said out loud.

"Don't tell who what?" said a cobra guard who had just come on the ledge.

Mandihar composed himself, quickly changing the subject.

"You all rested for your shift?"

"Yes, Grand Wizard. Just checking in."

Mandihar informed the guard of the new name added to the list before waving him off, watching him hurry down the path. He returned his cold, black eyes to the meadow, making sure all his other cobra patrol guards were in place for the night.

No garter living in Moon Meadow today could remember when their leader was a garter. Tales from those times told of a close community who enjoyed the freedom to gather, travel, and speak one's mind. If their leader wasn't doing a good job, they could replace him. Their dens were in a beautiful meadow with a river running through it, and they worked hard together to have a good life.

And suddenly everything changed. The garter leader disappeared and was never seen or heard from again, which sent shock waves of fear in his descendants down through the decades. In his place as leader came Mandihar, a huge cobra from another land whispered to be across the great water, who demanded to be called the Grand Wizard. The gurgling river still ran through the lush meadow, but life had changed dramatically in the garter dens.

Once a month, Mandihar allowed families to ignore the curfew and gather at the edge of the river to watch the moon's huge, silvery orb rise above the distant mountains and cast its beautiful glow on the river.

These mysterious nights were for storytelling and always went late while the moon climbed to the top of the heavens and started to slip down the other side. Mandihar smirked with satisfaction at the thought of his favorite story, one that frightened all the young snakes, and even some of the older ones. He had chosen a respectable snake of the community, Vasuki, to end the night with this specific tale. A low chuckle floated over the ledge as Mandihar envisioned Vasuki puffing up his chest before he began speaking. All the snakes' coils would tighten, eager with fear and anticipation, as the moonlight glittered off the multiple colors and patterns of their backs. The air would fill with a unison of soft, low hisses.

Vasuki spoke slowly, allowing each word to sink in as the tale would begin:

"If you follow the Snake River for miles, you will come upon a huge, forbidden rock tower called Kukulkan. It stands in an enormous crater of parched sand and dirt where nothing grows and the sun is merciless. Here the river turns sharply to the west as if its pure waters do not want to even touch this evil place. Bones litter the barren earth, and much of the time black buzzards hover overhead. Even the beautiful prairie grasses are afraid to enter, for they suddenly end with a steep drop-off into this cursed area, haunted by ancient spirits and an immortal creature known as HOXD: an enormous python with legs and arms and extraordinary magical powers. There are many ancient stories about this place, mostly rumors and myths. But no living creature we know of has ever been there and come back to tell the tale."

Deep breaths followed by slow hisses would erupt from the crowd.

"HOXD must replenish his energy every month by basking in the power of the full moon's light. It is essential that direct moonlight shines on the bare skin of his legs. Otherwise, his energy will not be restored, and his legs will revert to being a snake's tail. If this happens, he will become like all other mortals and eventually die."

Loud, excitable hissing would break out but quickly stop, allowing Vasuki to continue in an eerie voice.

"HOXD only leaves his den when the moon is full, so tonight, as I speak these words, he should be emerging. Using his magic, maybe from that tall tower, he can even see us!"

The nervous slithering and hissing would become so loud that Vasuki would have trouble settling it down. Eventually, he would be able to end the story with the same line he always used:

"Only the unwise would attempt to enter Kukulkan, for to access the tower and HOXD, one must travel on the Avenue of the Dead!"

The night would become ghostly silent as all the snakes sat transfixed by the images conjured in their minds by the thought of HOXD and Kukulkan.

CHAPTER 3

HISTORY WITH
MISS HISSY

G aia sat looking out of the school window, daydreaming. Two cobra patrols slithered by on the front path as she thought back to the times her dad had told exciting stories of the heavens and Earth and all the snake ancestors who lived before them. Today, however, she was stuck in Miss Hissy's history class, forced to listen to her droning on about the history of Moon Meadow.

Dominating the front of the classroom was a large lapis lazuli stone which, in certain lights, shone in a beautiful blue. A well-known older snake artist in the community had etched into the stone a likeness of the Grand Wizard Mandi-har. Before class started each morning, the students bowed to their leader. Below this was a wide slab of white calcite that Miss Hissy used for her daily lessons, etching them into the stone with a special tool she held with her tail. Today there was a horizontal line divided into five sections lettered from A to E. Lateral lines below each letter were divided into sections numbered from 1 to 6. None of the students had any idea what it meant.

Gaia was examining the lesson when she felt an intense stare from Kimba, who sat to her right next to Lucima. Casually, she turned her head, pretending to look out the door. Two huge, soft eyes met hers. Butterflies filled her stomach.

Be casual, Gaia, be casual, she thought to herself as she gave a slight smile while her heart raced.

As Miss Hissy's boring lecture droned on, she felt a poke on her side as Lucima passed her a note. Gaia waited for Miss Hissy to slither over to the other side of the class before she read it.

"Kimba is watching you!"

Excitement overtook Gaia as she tried to suppress her giggle; a small squeak came out.

Miss Hissy froze.

"Well, Gaia, do you have something to share with the class?"

"No, Miss Hissy."

Miss Hissy gave Gaia a questioning look for some time before continuing. Gaia felt paralyzed. Now Miss Hissy would be watching her and would intercept any notes going back and forth—and *read them to the entire class.* She felt frustrated and squirmed on her mat.

Miss Hissy finished her lecture as she slithered to the lesson stone in front of the class.

"Before I take questions, I must tell you about an order that Grand Wizard Mandihar has issued today. She pointed with her tail to the horizontal line on the stone.

"As of today, while in school all students will be assigned a code to use instead of their names. It will help with record keeping and will diffuse complaints against teachers being biased toward a student's name. Now you will be just a code."

Gaia's eyes grew wide with astonishment as they met Lucima's. Miss Hissy continued to explain the coding system as she pointed to the lesson stone. A letter designated which row a student sat in, and a number designated their place in that row. Miss Hissy instructed all the students to look down at their mats. Gaia now noticed that each space had lines etched in the floor. Miss Hissy explained that each student's mat had to be *exactly* centered within those lines to present a picture of perfect order. She went on as if this were completely normal and ended her lesson by stating that Mandihar had pronounced there would be no questions.

"I will, however, take questions on my lecture about Moon Meadow. Are there any?"

Gaia was still reeling from what she had just heard, but she immediately raised her tail. Miss Hissy glided back and forth on the floor in front of the class, scanning the perplexed faces of the students as she spoke. Even though she was keeping an eye on Gaia, she somehow seemed to miss her tail. Gaia sat up straighter, scales extended, stretching high into the air. The bright-blue stripe wiggled frantically. A loud, exasperated sigh came from Miss Hissy.

"Yes, Gaia, do you have a question?" she said precisely.

Somewhat slowly, Gaia tucked her tail neatly underneath her.

"Yes, Miss Hissy. Kukulkan is very old—"

Miss Hissy irately interrupted before Gaia asked her question. "That's right."

"But how come we can't go there?" Gaia asked.

Miss Hissy stopped and looked directly at Gaia. All her fine wrinkles became accentuated as her eyes narrowed.

"That is not important," Miss Hissy said, intent on continuing her lecture.

"Why is it not important?"

Miss Hissy's mouth tightened. She slithered over to Gaia, leaning down within millimeters of her little snake face. Slowly and loudly, Miss Hissy answered.

"I said it is not important!"

Gaia backed up a hair and squirmed slightly on her mat, knowing she should stop talking, but right now, having been downgraded to a code, she was feeling more feisty than usual and continued.

"I don't understand, Miss Hissy. If this is history class, why is something in the past not important?"

Deafening silence filled the classroom. All eyes were on Miss Hissy, waiting for her eruptive response. Miss Hissy threw her head back and began slithering in short, frantic bursts back and forth.

"What is important, Gaia, is that Mandihar says Kukulkan is forbidden to all inhabitants of Moon Meadow."

No one uttered a word.

"Now let's move on, shall we?"

Gaia slightly nodded her head in agreement. Miss Hissy straightened her posture; her forced smile did not match her hard black eyes.

"Let's see, where was I . . . "

A soft voice interrupted again. "But why is it forbidden?"

Miss Hissy's anger could no longer be suppressed. Her voice grew a few octaves higher than usual as she yelled, "That's it, E6! Go sit out there!" Her tail pointed stiffly to the hallway. "Immediately!"

Gaia looked around, having no idea who Miss Hissy was screaming at.

"E6, I said go sit in the hallway!"

Gaia continued to stay coiled on her mat, totally bewildered at what was going on. When she looked at Miss Hissy, the teacher was charging down the aisle with a face so vicious it scared Gaia. She came to an abrupt halt next to Gaia's mat, spittle gathering at the corners of her mouth as she screamed.

"You are out of line, E6," Miss Hissy shouted like a maniac. "And sit up tall and look at me when I'm speaking."

Gaia stretched up as far as she could and looked at Miss Hissy, having no idea why she was screaming. Then something clicked in her brain. She was E6.

It seemed Miss Hissy had gone insane with the bit of new power Mandihar's mandate gave her. "Go! Sit! In! The! Hallway!"

Gaia slowly got off her mat and slithered down the aisle to the front of the class, who continued to look on with their mouths open. She met Miss Hissy's icy stare and forced herself to not look away.

Once in the hallway, she curled up in a coil at the side of the doorway and tried to stop her heart's pounding . . . She lay her head down on the rough dirt and watched her classmates.

Everyone's eyes followed Miss Hissy's movements. Everyone's except for Kimba's; he kept his gaze on Gaia the entire time.

Miss Hissy instructed her class to read chapter 8 as she crept to her desk and dug out Mandihar's *Guidance Manual for Young Snake Minds*. She tried calming herself by turning to chapter 10, verse 2: "How to Break a Strong-Willed Snake." In the *Manual*, Mandihar had included a page on which teachers were required to list the names of troublesome students. Gaia's name was on that list many times, and now Miss Hissy added her name again, E6.

CHAPTER 4

BROTHER AND LEG WALKERS

Not long after Gaia's run-in with Miss Hissy, in the early evening hours of what had been a beautiful summer day, it was just Gaia and her brother, Pharaoh, coiled in the reeds by the river. They had always loved to coil in the tall, cool grass on the bank of the Snake River that ran close to their family den. Ever since they could remember, they would coil up next to their mom and dad on nights when the moon was full and watch it rise. In the distance, they would see Mandihar sitting on his ledge. As they got older, this would really irritate Pharaoh; he was sick of being small and drab, with his bland brown scales and tan stripes. He hated how Mandihar literally looked down on them. He hated that he couldn't fight back. He became angrier the older he got, the more he'd heard tell of their past—yet it was never enough, tales full of secrets and unanswered questions. Yet he did not dare speak against Mandihar, at least not out loud.

They were old enough now to go to the river alone and always laughed when their parents told them not to go far from the den. They were told to be on the lookout for owls that scouted the area at night and loved young snakes for their snacks. Pharaoh scoffed at the thought. He was almost an adult and could get away from or defeat some stupid owl. Vasuki always told Pharaoh to watch out for Gaia, at which point Chu'mana, their mom, would always break into the conversation and firmly say, "Females are perfectly capable of looking after themselves."

The moon wasn't yet full, but it was the last time that Gaia and Pharaoh would sit together in this place they loved, for tomorrow was Pharaoh's fifteenth birthday. When a male snake reached young adulthood, Mandihar had established a ritual celebration held in the foothills of his mountain retreat. This "welcome to adulthood" celebration marked the soon-to-be beginning of the young adult's long training with the wizard in the ancient traditions and beliefs of his ancestors.

These celebrations were famous for their many activities and delicacies. Gaia's favorite game, Search for Serpens, was played when the night became totally dark. The huge expanse of black sky shone brightly with millions of stars, and in that mysterious realm everyone competed to be the first to locate the constellation of Serpens, which was the snake world's connection to the heavens. Excited chatter always erupted among the young snakes, as they all wanted to be the first to locate it. Once all the snakes could identify the shape of a serpent in the stars, the stories began. She and Pharaoh loved letting their imaginations run rampant.

"Are you nervous about your birthday?" Gaia asked, turning in the reeds to look at Pharaoh in the peaceful, dusky light.

Pharaoh hesitated a bit and then said, "Kinda. Mandihar sorta freaks me out. I don't know what to expect."

"Yeah, he is pretty creepy, especially with those huge yellow fangs." Gaia shuddered at the thought.

Pharaoh laughed at his sister's reaction. "At the same time, I wanna hear what he has to say about stuff."

"Like what?"

"Like, what happened way back when . . . you know, like why do the Leg Walkers hate us so much? That kinda stuff."

"I wonder why these initiations are just for males? And why can't anyone talk about it afterward?" Gaia always got frustrated when she thought about the unfairness of it all. Why should Pharoah get to have the initiation ritual and the training? She was completely capable of learning the ancient ways and wisdoms.

"Well, that goes back thousands of years," Pharaoh said with certainty, sounding like a text slab from Miss Hissy's class. "Females obviously aren't as strong as males, and their brains just work differently. They can't grasp the hard concepts. They do better at simpler tasks, like cleaning. I am not sure who said that, but it makes sense to me."

Gaia sat staring at him in disbelief as he continued. "You know, all Mom does is sweep the garden path. And all that the girl snakes seem to care about is who has the prettiest scales and who their current best friend is."

Gaia loved Pharaoh, but when he got like this, she didn't even *like* him. She was ready to go to war with him.

"Oh, my Serpens! Do you really believe that?" she shouted.

"Well look, Gaia. When Dad tells those stupid stories about Kukulkan and HOXD and ancestors who had legs and arms, you just soak it up! Do you really believe that? It makes absolutely no sense."

"Just because it doesn't make sense to your pea-size brain doesn't mean it couldn't exist—or doesn't exist," Gaia shouted even louder. She was frantically slithering in a circle to relieve her agitation.

"You're such a—"

Pharaoh abruptly stopped speaking and was completely still as approaching footsteps resounded in the earth. Both snakes tightened their coils simultaneously at the sound of danger. Heavy footsteps shook the ground as they drew closer. Gaia caught a glimpse of two large black boots approaching her and her brother.

Their differences evaporated as danger approached and Pharaoh whispered to Gaia, "Oh no, it's the Leg Walkers!"

Gaia shuddered. A slow, low hiss escaped her mouth. Loud voices spoke directly above them, seeming to come from the heavens. Gaia said a small prayer to Serpens, pleading with the higher being to make the Leg Walkers just move past without noticing her and her brother. But the big black boots stopped right above them.

"That was some great hunting, no?"

"Totally. Those rabbits are big mothers."

Gaia peered at the two men through the leaves she lay beneath. They each carried a line of some sort with a huge, lifeless rabbit attached to it. Both wore funny, multi-green-and brown-colored outfits with matching hats and big rifles slung over their shoulders. She had seen these costumes before; she thought they looked ridiculous. A loud burp pierced the pure air, startling Gaia and Pharaoh. The taller Leg Walker took one last swig of his beer as the two of them started to walk off.

Suddenly, a shiny silver object came hurtling toward Gaia, barely missing her head. A loud hiss came from behind. Gaia quickly looked over and saw her brother's back split open with a stream of blood beginning to seep from the wound.

The Leg Walkers came to a halt.

"Hey man, there's two snakes right there," one said, pointing as they both slowly began stepping backward.

Pharaoh's brown scales pulsated as he slithered back and forth in pain. Gaia's eyes locked in on the Leg Walker's soulless brown eyes. She tried intimidating them with a deep warning hiss as she thrust herself toward them.

The Leg Walker grabbed a large stick in the weeds..

"Hey, move over. I'm gonna kill those nasty creatures," he said to his buddy, who snorted.

"Yeah, man, kill 'em! I hate snakes!"

They laughed. One said, "Maybe we can stuff them and put them on our wall."

"Nah," the other one answered. "No one puts a snake on their trophy wall. They're too disgusting!"

Gaia whisper-screamed at her brother. "We gotta get outta here now!"

Pharaoh moaned in agreement. Gaia pointed with the tip of her tail.

"Over there, under those rocks."

Pharaoh's adrenaline kicked in, giving him the strength to slither to safety. Gaia followed right behind.

"Get those filthy things," a voice shouted.

The tall Leg Walker started to run toward them, screaming as he lifted the stick above his head, holding it still for a split second in striking position.

Gaia shrieked, "Hurry up, Pharaoh!"

The attacker began swinging the stick downward when he stumbled on the uneven terrain, flying forward and losing his grip on the stick. A loud thud hit the dirt trail inches behind Gaia's tail.

Pharaoh and Gaia dove their heads down into the small pile of rock, their wiggling bodies squirming in quickly.

Loud curses faded as Gaia and Pharaoh lay quietly on the cool dirt of the small enclosure, waiting for the Leg Walkers to leave.

"Here, you drive." The big Leg Walker, who was limping, hollered to his buddy many steps ahead of him. He tossed his buddy the keys to an old, badly rusted pick-up truck that was parked in the grass on the side of the dirt road. He threw his gun and the dead rabbit in the bed of the truck and opened the passenger door. Empty beer cans and chip bags rolled out onto the grass, and he gave them a kick with his good leg, sending them flying into the ditch.

"I twisted my ankle real good back there," the big guy said as he pulled himself into the truck and slammed the door.

"Them snakes is always waitin' in the grass to get ya," the driver said as he accelerated fast, sending gravel and dust flying in the air.

"Next time we will get them first!"

Gaia and Pharaoh waited until the loud, rattling engine grew distant before emerging out into the open and heading home. The slithering motion caused Pharaoh's wound to bleed heavily, forcing them to stop in the tall grasses. Gaia scanned the surrounding area until she found the exact towering plant she needed. Quickly, she plucked a finely divided leaf from its stem and applied it to her brother's back. The bleeding stopped instantly.

CHAPTER 5

BACK HOME AND BACK OUT AGAIN

Pharaoh and Gaia slid quickly down the entry shaft into their den, startling their parents and grandparents. They were gathered in the large area at the bottom, just enjoying each other's company and reminiscing about earlier days when Gaia and Pharaoh were young and life seemed more carefree.

The elders looked with concern at Pharaoh and Gaia, who were both covered in dirt and blood.

"That wasn't an owl, was it?" Vasuki said, trying to make a joke to lighten the tension.

But Pharaoh wasn't in a humorous mood. "Does it look like something a bird would do?" he said with anger.

Vasuki was taken aback at Pharaoh's abruptness. Pharaoh's grandpa warned him, "Be careful of your tone when you speak to your father."

Pharaoh just stared at both with angry eyes. The wound on his back burned and hurt.

"What happened?" Chu'mana asked her daughter.

"The Leg Walkers from the hunting camp tried to kill us for no reason. We barely got away."

Pharaoh's breathing was raspy and agitated, but he didn't say anything. There was an unfamiliar tension between Pharaoh and his father.

"Is there anything you'd like to add, Pharaoh?" Vasuki asked his son.

"Oh yeah," Pharaoh said, "but it's nothing any of you would want to hear."

"Try us!" his grandfather said, surprised to see Pharaoh's level of anger.

Pharaoh stared directly at his father as he answered. "My friends and I decided we are not putting up with this anymore. Gaia and I were almost killed by Leg Walkers who hate us for no reason. Next time I am fighting back."

Vasuki gave Pharaoh a stern look and said, "I don't see that you've grown bigger or more poisonous, so what do you plan to do?"

Pharaoh looked defiantly at his father. "We have relatives who are huge, and some are very poisonous. We'll get them to help us and let those Leg Walkers know to leave us alone . . . or we'll die trying!"

Pharaoh saw concern in the eyes of his mother. His grandfather just looked shocked. Pharaoh felt conflicted for an instant, but he knew he couldn't take it back. In the silence that followed, Chu'mana left the room and came back with Mandihar's *Manual*. She scrolled her tail down the rock slab to chapter 7, verse 5: "How to Deal with Belligerent Youth." She placed it in front of Vasuki, who glanced at it briefly.

Vasuki took a deep breath and said, "Tomorrow you will meet with Mandihar and—"

"I know, I know, Dad. He'll teach me about our glorious history and how our species has always followed the path of peace."

"Maybe you should respect your elders and listen to what he has to say."

"Has it ever occurred to you that Mandihar is a *cobra*? One of the most poisonous and feared creatures on the Earth. I bet Leg Walkers don't pick on *him*. But he teaches us to be all wimpy and to accept being killed. No more, Dad, no more!"

"Pharaoh, could we talk ab—"

"No, Dad, we can't."

The whole family was stunned. Pharaoh had had episodes of attitude, but nothing like this before.

Pharoah caught Gaia's eye and somehow felt she understood. In the blink of an eye, Pharoah steeled himself against the pain in his back and slithered up the access shaft. He went into the tall grasses and turned in the opposite direction from what he usually took. When his family finally emerged into the gathering dark, Pharaoh was long gone.

31

CHAPTER 6

ON THE WAY TO THE CELEBRATION

The grasses were still wet with dew in the valley of Moon Meadow as the sun surmounted the mountains and shone on the caravan of snakes heading toward the foothills of the Atum Mountains, where the great celebration of Pharaoh's fifteenth birthday was to take place. Despite the events of the previous evening, Gaia and her parents had joined their neighbor snakes in making their way to the party.

The group of snakes slowed down as they approached each den along the way and the inhabitants fell into line. No snake stayed home on this day. Well, almost no snake.

Asmodeus was a crotchety old snake who lived next door to Grandma and Grandpa. Even though he was old, he was in good shape and could have joined the group, but he never left his den. According to the rumors of Moon Meadow, he disliked everyone.

There was a story from long ago of a snake who had seen

Asmodeus outside his den one night, but only briefly. The snake telling the story said it was as if Asmodeus sensed he was being watched and hurried back into his den. His slither was not normal, though; it was more like a slither in the front and a hopping motion in the back. No one could say for sure.

The caravan began to pass Asmodeus's den, but they all knew too well that he would never come out, so they did not even slow down. None of them, that is, except Gaia, who brought her slither down to a crawl as she squinted her eyes to catch a glimpse into Asmodeus's window, just a hole in his hillside den. As usual, in front of the window was a small pile of rocks to block the sun from entering. Gaia felt disappointed at the sight, even though it was the same sight she had seen throughout her entire life. Although she had never witnessed any signs of life at his den, she always held a glimmer of hope as she approached that maybe this would be the day Asmodeus would join the Moon Meadow snake world. Sometimes Gaia would envision him gorging on a plateful of baked ants, but deep down she knew it was just wishful thinking. She wondered what he did all day, alone in the dark. She was almost past his den when she swore one of the rocks in front of the window shifted. She stopped abruptly, causing her mother to run into her headfirst.

"Gaia, what are you doing?" Chu'mana went into an uncontrollable sneezing fit.

"Sorry, Mom. I thought I saw something in the window."

"Oh, Gaia, will you leave that poor old snake alone?" Chu'mana said between sneezes.

"I am just so curious about him, though. Aren't you?"

Chu'mana ignored her daughter's question. "Come on now. Your brother is waiting for us."

Chu'mana's sneezing stopped as she picked up her pace to catch up to the rest of the group. Gaia snuck one last glance as she began to slither. There it was again—one of the rocks shifted slightly. She halted immediately. Chu'mana continued her fast pace to catch up with the caravan. The rocks slowly moved back and forth, small specks of dirt and sand falling down the hillside. The stones jostled a few more times, creating a small opening between them. Gaia sat motionless as she watched. Suddenly, the space was filled again, but this time not with a rock. No, there was an eye staring directly at her, but not a normal snake eye. This one was different. It sat between Asmodeus's two brown eyes, right smack in the middle. The third eye shone bright purple with a half-hung, lazy, wrinkled eyelid draping over it. Gaia felt like the wind had been knocked out of her. She inhaled deeply to help calm the uneasiness rising inside her. Their eyes remained fixed on each other. Before Gaia could even think, the eyes were gone, disappearing as quickly as they had come. A few movements of the rocks and then the den window appeared as usual: dark and blocked off. Gaia slithered to catch up with her family faster than she had ever slithered in her life.

Gaia caught up to her mom just as they approached the next den, the home of her grandparents who had returned late last night in a very agitated state.

"Mom, I . . . I . . ."

Chu'mana looked over at her breathless daughter. "What's wrong, honey?"

"I saw something back there at Asmodeus's den."

Chu'mana's genuine concern vanished into irritation. "Oh Gaia, not this again. I told you to leave that poor snake alone."

"But Mom, I saw him! He had a strange purple third eye—"

Chu'mana cut her daughter off. "Gaia, stop with your tales. You always let your imagination get the best of you, and you are getting too old for that!"

"But Mom, he had an extra eye! And it was purple with a creepy dried-out eyelid hanging over it! It was scary looking!"

"Gaia, stop it right now. It was probably the sun's reflection. There's nothing different about that old snake."

Chu'mana kept pace with the others as Gaia fell back slightly. She felt the same defeat she'd felt when speaking to Miss Hissy. She knew what she had seen, and it was not a trick of the sun's reflection. It was real. Asmodeus had a terrifying purple third eye that sent shivers down her spine. Gaia's thoughts were interrupted as her grandparents joined the caravan, blending in with the group of snakes heading toward the mountain. Her grandma made sure she was next to Gaia.

"How is my beautiful granddaughter this morning?" she said to Gaia. "Last evening, I was looking forward to talking to you and catching up on everything that is happening in your life; and then it turned out so different . . . so sad."

Grandma paused. "You were almost killed, Gaia. I almost lost you."

Her voice cracked as she continued. "I can't even think about it. It made me think we don't see each other as often anymore as we did when you were little ormrs and Grandpa and I would often look after you and Pharaoh."

"What are ormrs, Grandma?" she asked giggling.

"Why, ormrs are young snakes or serpents. They're not called that anymore?" her grandma asked in mock surprise.

"You know they're not, Grandma." The old snake laughed softly as she sidled up to her granddaughter and continued moving forward in rhythm with her head touching Gaia's.

The caravan was drawing close to the mountain. Grandma stretched her head high into the air as all the individual dens broke up and began mingling with neighbors and old friends. Gaia noticed her grandma's eyes nervously scanning the crowd.

"What's wrong, Grandma?"

"Oh, Grandpa wanted to talk to your dad and mom about a problem . . . Some young males behaving aggressively, especially towards Leg Walkers. After Pharaoh's comments last night, Grandpa is worried. I spotted your grandfather, but I don't see Pharaoh anywhere."

Gaia wondered where her brother was hiding as her grandma continued.

"You know, Pharaoh might not agree with Mandihar, but he will learn a great deal from him during his initiation."

"Pharaoh will be fine," Gaia said, but for a split second she heard his words of last night and wasn't sure he would be.

"Well, my dear granddaughter, we haven't had much chance to talk, but we certainly will during these next few days." Grandma kissed Gaia on the face as her husband approached with Chu'mana and Vasuki.

By now almost all the serpents had gone into the foot-hills where the activities were starting. Gaia and her family held back so that Pharaoh would see them, but he never came.

Surprised and saddened, they scanned the huge crowd, finding it impossible to believe that he wouldn't show up. Finally, Gaia spotted Pharaoh with a group of young males. She noticed her grandpa flash a worried look to her dad, but her concern was fleeting.

"Oh, there's Lucima," Gaia said excitedly.

She yelled Lucima's name loudly so she would be heard above the rising din of excited garters. Lucima's whole family turned around, but then her father and brothers continued gliding toward the ballfield. Lucima and her mother waited for Gaia's family to come to them.

"Oh my," Lucima's mom said to Gaia as she approached. "That yell was loud enough to challenge any male snake." She wasn't smiling.

Gaia was taken aback, and before she could say anything, Lucima's mom turned to Chu'mana.

"Hello, darling, how *are* you? It's been far too long." Then, as a condescending afterthought, she offhandedly greeted the rest of the family.

"Mom," Lucima interrupted, "can Gaia and I go with Dad to the flickball game?"

Her mother let out a heavy sigh.

"No, of course not. That's for the boys. There are plenty of nice events for girls. Why don't you and Gaia go check out a cooking demonstration or a snakelet care class?"

Gaia shot her mother a look of horrified desperation.

"Well, can I have some more mambas to buy some spider-cream?" Lucima asked.

Lucima's mom rolled her eyes as she sifted through her

purse with her tail.

"Here, you can have two mambas, but make sure you share with your friend."

Lucima and Gaia smiled as they took the yellow pebbles and coiled in the sun, patiently waiting for their parents to finish their conversation.

Lucima's mother turned to Chu'mana.

"You must be *so* proud of Pharaoh on this day. We saw that he arrived with some of his new friends. I certainly hope you were able to speak to him before he begins his initiation," she said with false concern.

Chu'mana started to respond, but Lucima's mom cut her off.

"Well, I must hurry on. I'm working in the Mothers for Mandihar booth. I haven't seen you at any of the meetings, and we miss you. Ta-ta!"

She wiggled away quickly, disappearing into the crowd.

Chu'mana and Vasuki just looked at each other in irritated bewilderment. Then Chu'mana said, "Is she for real?"

Vasuki looked affectionately at his wife. "I think she is stuck back in time . . . like fifty years ago."

Gaia and Lucima snickered as they headed towards the spidercream stand.

Mandihar made his majestic appearance, sitting tall on a high rock ledge. A hushed silence descended on the excited crowd below who now turned to their leader and bowed. A rather long silence prevailed before Mandihar gave the opening words of his traditional short speech.

"Welcome my beloved snakes of Moon Meadow and all surrounding communities! Once again, we gather to celebrate a young snake's passage into adulthood and all that that entails: a life of service in the leadership of the International Snake Council or a more conventional family life of equitable devotion to the mandates of the Council on an always-level playing field."

Pharaoh was with his friends in the crowd below, wanting to wait until the last minute to join Mandihar on the ledge. Pharoah turned to them. "Same speech every time, even though no one really knows what he means."

"And, of course, no one ever asks," one of them said with a laugh.

"Not in Moon Meadow."

Mandihar continued, "Now is the time to celebrate. Eat all you like, play any game you desire . . . just enjoy yourselves. It's all taken care of by those who watch over you."

Mandihar slithered back a bit, indicating his speech was over. The crowd politely applauded by beating their tails on the ground, then scattered in all directions to start the celebration with joyous hissing.

Pharaoh was not allowed to partake in the celebration; Mandihar did not want his mind and body overstimulated and clouded by too much food and drink. Slowly, Pharaoh began his climb up the long stone ramp that wound its way around the mountain. Today it was festooned with brightly colored flowers from the meadow. Their delicate beauty stood out starkly against the mountain's foreboding, dark granite walls. As he ascended, Pharaoh felt something he had never experienced before. As the raucous sounds of his fellow garters celebrating below faded, the sky seemed bluer, the sun brighter and warmer, the air purer, while at the same time it was a bit more difficult to breathe. Running through his mind were snippets of conversations among the elders, which he had overheard growing up—talk of ancient times and creatures of the earth who strove to understand their connection to the heavens. He stopped several times to absorb that feeling, a feeling that he could do anything.

As Pharaoh rounded the last curve, there sat Mandihar with his face to the sun in a beautiful, large mountaintop meadow of red and yellow flowers and huge white desert lilies. All were interspersed with green plants and set among huge stones with mysterious carvings. Pharaoh startled a bit when he saw numerous garters tending the plants. One snake raised his head and looked directly at Pharaoh, who almost gasped audibly when he saw the face of a classmate who had disappeared years ago while playing in the fields of Moon Meadow. The story was that he had been killed by a Leg Walker. Their eyes locked for an instant, and then the worker quickly lowered his head.

Mandihar turned to look at Pharaoh just then, his gaze intense.

"Garters are good workers. They tend my garden well," was all Mandihar said.

Mandihar then turned to observe with cold, cruel eyes what appeared from this height to be very small, insignificant celebrants in the valley below. He laughed inside at how all of Moon Meadow's inhabitants were oblivious to the real reason for these initiations. All they saw was a time to look forward to, a coming together and party for everyone.

However, Mandihar knew the truth. The fact was that he was really looking for the perfect male garter snake who would be receptive to his ideas and assist him in keeping Moon Meadow under control. It was always the young males who presented the greatest threat to his absolute rule, and that threat was becoming greater by the day. He forced a smile at his new initiate, wondering whether this could finally be the one.

Pharaoh bowed before the Grand Wizard. Then, together they disappeared into his inner sanctum.

CHAPTER 7

ASMODEUS'S ANGER

Earlier, Asmodeus had watched from behind the rocks covering his window as the last of the long line of festive garters glided by. He always wondered what the reason for these group gatherings was but was too afraid to find out. His mind drifted to when he still had his garter family. Back then there were five of them. Asmodeus thought of his one brother who had left home very early, standing tall and muscular with well-developed arms and legs, never to be heard from again. Unlike other families in Moon Meadow, none of Asmodeus's siblings had any recollection of any family. He felt as if one day they had just dropped down from the heavens, not as blessed beings but as monstrous, scary creatures to be avoided. Today, he felt alone.

Asmodeus looked down at his undeveloped legs. When he moved, it was slither-hop, slither-hop, not just slither. He recalled how all his siblings had the same deformity. Plus, his sister had one vestigial arm. And worst of all, Asmodeus and his brother had three eyes—two normal ones and a purple third eye, right in the middle. Asmodeus always thought of himself as strange but didn't realize to what extent until the caravan of snakes began passing his window every year.

Asmodeus longed for his loving siblings who always watched out for one another. His heart sank as he remembered the night he lost his sister and brother. The memory felt fresh as he relived the pain all over again. When his siblings had not returned home from searching for food, he went out looking for them. A wave of emotion swept thorough Asmodeus at the thought of their lifeless bodies lying next to scattered stones. Immediately he knew who was responsible.

"Filthy Leg Walkers," Asmodeus called out to his empty den. The travel down memory lane continued to when it was just he and his one brother who remained. Both had developed a yearning to be out of their den when the moon was full. Asmodeus never understood why he had such a compulsion, only that an unexplainable feeling of empowerment came with the moonlight and then baffling energy during thunderstorms.

Asmodeus began slithering around his den, attempting to fight back the overwhelming sadness. Bright bolts of light filled his mind as he recalled the night that he and his brother with the third eye felt omnipotent. All of Moon Meadow had safely tucked themselves away in their dens as Mother Nature unleashed a powerful storm. Overcome by euphoria, Asmodeus and his brother ventured out into the pelting rain and soon encountered a large rock that loomed in front of them. A dull throb formed behind Asmodeus' purple eye as he recalled using his powers for the first time. Somehow, he had managed to levitate the enormous rock five feet into the air. His brother was exuberant at the feat and slithered underneath for fun. Asmodeus's tail slapped hard against the dirt as he tried keeping his emotions at bay. For years he had suppressed all thoughts of that night, but his mind no longer allowed it, and the image of a huge stone crashing down rushed into view. He could almost feel the spray of mud on his face as the memory of what was left of his brother flashed before him: the tip of his tail. Asmodeus circled around his room in agony.

"Why . . . Why?" he yelled.

An uncontrollable shudder surged through his body as the realization set in that he was completely alone in this world. The day had slipped away, and the slanting rays of the setting sun were now shining through his small window. There was a slight breeze and on it he heard the distant sounds of merriment from the celebration. He felt a great need to know who and what he and his family were. He felt sadness for all those who were different and reviled. And then he felt anger. Searing, burning, explosive frustration and anger. And he left his den to spy on the parade.

CHAPTER 8

PHARAOH'S INITIATION & THE GOLDEN TABLET

Pharaoh exhibited an air of total confidence as he followed Mandihar up the mountain, with the huge gathering of snakes from the surrounding area cheering and sending prayers heavenward from the valley below. He caught a glimpse of his family in the throng, and a pang of guilt shot through his body.

However, it was a sense of dread and near panic that swept through Pharaoh when they were alone inside. He realized that this was the first time he had ever been up close to Mandihar, whose very large size overwhelmed him. Every snake in the valley knew he could kill almost instantly with one bite, but being right next to him magnified Pharaoh's sense of helplessness.

Mandihar's black scales were offset by vibrant yellow crossbands. Two cold, seemingly lifeless eyes sat deep in his large head. Two long, hollow, yellowish fangs hanging out of his mouth grabbed Pharaoh's attention; he knew that at any moment venom could flow through them.

The room they entered was huge, with openings in the high ceiling through which shafts of sunlight glinted off big, sculpted stones with strange engravings that Pharaoh had never seen before. Comfortable mats of woven reeds were placed in a circle, with a raised mat in the middle. Along the far edge of the room were several entries to other areas of the cave. A slight, sweet-smelling haze filled the room, and soon Pharaoh started to relax. From the far corner of the room, a female cobra entered and quietly dropped off a selection of toads, tree frogs, and baby mice. She placed them in front of Mandihar and silently left the room. Mandihar leaned in closer to Pharaoh and whispered, "These were seasoned with herbs from my garden." Pharaoh's eyes followed her, but now he was so relaxed he didn't really care what was going on. He only knew he felt quite drowsy, and everything seemed surreal. Suddenly, every little thing was hilarious, and Pharaoh erupted in uncontainable laughter. Between these bouts of hilarity, Pharaoh coiled on one of the mats. Mandihar was already coiled on his elevated platform and had begun speaking.

" . . . and the main idea you should take from our days together should be one that speaks to power . . . "

Pharaoh's laughter ceased. He didn't think he had heard Mandihar's words properly. They were totally contrary to what he had been taught all his life. He groggily raised his head higher to get some focus.

The old wizard took notice of this and came off his perch. He carefully selected one of the mice that lay before him and pushed it toward Pharaoh.

"It seems you're hungry. Eat this," he said softly, in an almost fatherly way. "It will make you feel better and a bit more alert."

Mandihar seemed to have a certain warmth until Pharaoh looked in his eyes, which were cold and predatory. The haze in the room had disappeared. The setting sun shone through the openings in the roof and focused directly on Mandihar, who sat fully upright with his hood extended. Mandihar's eyes scared Pharaoh, and he trembled, totally unaware of what was to come.

They sat in silence for some time while Pharaoh's head cleared a bit, and he was able to focus again. Total relaxation replaced his fear, almost to the point of not caring about anything.

Mandihar analyzed Pharaoh's every movement and reaction. He was growing weary of all the failed initiations. He desperately needed to find a garter to make second-in-command, and time was of the essence.

Mandihar knew he was only a link in a chain of middle management and that the real power originated with an invisible group that had existed for millennia without ever being truly identified. His immediate contact was with the International Snake Council but above that, he had no idea who gave the orders.

Secrets, always secrets, he screamed in his mind.

Only one creature on Earth was known to hold at least some of those secrets: HOXD.

Mandihar began with his usual series of questions to determine the direction of the initiation. "How do you feel about Leg Walkers?"

"I hate them," Pharaoh said in a very forthright way.

Mandihar let out a laugh with a small grin. He had been watching Pharaoh since he arrived in Moon Meadow. Pharaoh was exceptionally bright and strong willed, and not aggressive by nature; however, Mandihar had heard stories that he was starting to fight back against the Leg Walkers. Throughout all the years of initiations, Mandihar had yet to come across such a feisty young snake. His informants told him Pharaoh was also openly hateful toward the injustices inflicted on Moon Meadow, but if he could harness that anger and manipulate it to work for his own good, he would have his second-in-command. Mandihar knew it was risky, but he had to try.

"What would you do to a captured Leg Walker?"

Without hesitation Pharaoh replied, "I would attack him." Pharaoh's eyes lit up at the thought and repeated it, louder. "I would attack him!"

A maniacal smile spread over Mandihar's face. He was a step closer to finally finding his initiate. He pushed another toad toward Pharaoh.

"Have another bite," he said as he sat back with satisfaction, his mind spinning with hope. He waited a few minutes before continuing. "What do you think of HOXD?"

Mandihar paused to let Pharaoh think for a moment.

Pharaoh groggily said in a slurred voice, "That's a stupid story my dad used to tell us. My sister always got scared. It's shtupid."

Mandihar was glad Pharaoh was hearing and comprehending what he was saying, but he warned Pharoah nonetheless. "I don't allow disrespect, but I will overlook it this time because I caused it. Now. Just pretend for a minute that HOXD is real. What would you do if you met him?" Mandihar asked.

"He has legs, doesn't he?"

Mandihar could hardly control himself with such insolence from an initiate, but he knew Pharaoh was the garter he had been looking for. He couldn't let this opportunity slip away.

During all the other initiations Mandihar would teach the mundane aspects of Moon Meadow's history, leaving out the secretive truth. He ended every session with the same warning: "Share even a little of this information and you will be severely punished."

Finally, he could now progress with the plan. He immediately summoned two of his cobra guards, who silently glided into the room. Pharaoh's eyes widened with Mandihar's sudden sense of urgency.

"Yes, Grand Wizard."

"Bring me the Golden Tablets."

Both guards hesitated. "The Golden Tablets, sir?"

"Did I stutter? Yes, the Golden Tablets!"

An uncomfortable silence hung in the air until the cobras returned.

One cobra grunted as he pulled a huge pile of golden tablets securely coiled in his tail, the other snake pushing behind him with all his might. Mandihar did not offer any assistance as he waited patiently for the pile to be released in front of him. Carefully, he brushed his large tail over the top of the pile, wiping away the dust of the centuries. He exuded uncontainable pleasure at the thought of finally being able to share the secrets that the Council had entrusted to him.

Mandihar paused and looked at Pharaoh, who appeared bewildered.

"I am going to tell you a story now," Mandihar finally said. "One that no snake knows because it is never taught. Look around this room. All these huge ancient stones covered with symbols that no one understands."

Mandihar began reading from the first tablet. Pharaoh sat up straighter.

> *"In the mists of unremembered days, there were two-legged creatures with strong rear limbs who walked upright on the Earth. They were not the human Leg Walkers we know today; those come much later. These were our ancestors, snakes who were very similar to some of their close lizard relatives."*

Mandihar paused to let this sink in. He knew Pharaoh's brain was still affected by his special seasoning. The old wizard was pleased with his confused reaction and continued.

> *"A beautifully preserved fossil of an ancient snake with fully developed rear limbs was unearthed and was believed to be about 95 million years old. A treasure trove of other similar*

*fossil skeletons was then discovered in the same area. Proof
that snakes once walked."*

Mandihar's eyes scrolled down the tablet.

*"... and there are many, many pictures and sculptures
and monuments and artifacts of serpents in sacred sites all
around the world. Many legends speak of the Serpent People,
a very intelligent race who were healers and taught the sci-
ence of mathematics and astronomy to what you think of as
the Leg Walkers ..."*

Mandihar looked up from his reading and asked, "This
story is nothing like what you were taught in school, is it?"

"No," Pharaoh finally said, still sounding groggy. "We
always learned that there are many examples all over the world
of ancient Leg Walkers worshipping the Serpent, but not about
the serpent having legs or anything else."

Pharaoh couldn't continue. He felt like screaming and
laughing hysterically at the same time. He didn't understand
what was happening to him.

Mandihar watched him carefully. "Is there anything else?"
he said.

"Oh, yes," Pharaoh said sarcastically. "We did learn that
these Serpent People taught the Leg Walkers to love and
respect each other and to not be violent." Pharaoh burst into
uncontrollable laughter and couldn't stop.

"And why is that funny?" Mandihar hissed.

Between convulsions of laughter, Pharaoh said, "Because

it makes no sense. We taught them to love and respect each other and to not be violent, and now they hate us—supposedly their teachers—and try to kill us on sight. What happened? Something major had to have happened. What was it? Why don't we know about it?"

Mandihar watched with cold eyes as his young initiate fell back exhausted and slipped into oblivion.

The thick cavern walls blocked out the sound of the celebration now in full swing in the foothills below. There were a few hours of daylight left before the commotion would start to settle down for the day. Mandihar sat on a reed cushion next to Pharaoh, hoping sleep would help him process what he had learned. This gave Mandihar time to figure out what to do with Pharaoh's inquisitive sister. His crew had warned him she was asking too many questions. He observed Pharaoh as he slept while constructing a plan. The festivities' participants below continued celebrating in blissful ignorance.

CHAPTER 9

ASMODEUS SPIES

Some snake families were leaving the celebration as Asmodeus arrived very cautiously, hanging back in the tall weeds
that surrounded the foothills. There were sights and sounds
that were totally unfamiliar to him. The bright light of the rising almost-full moon flashed like blinking lights off the skin of
hundreds of snakes still celebrating. Some were dancing, some
were singing, some young snakes in love had slithered into
the weeds to be alone. Some were still eating delicacies from
surrounding stands that were now closed, bearing signs like
"Baked Ants, All Varieties" and "Delicious Deep-Fried Toads."
Asmodeus was mesmerized by all he saw, but what impressed
him most was that as far as he could see, every snake was
accepted and seemed happy. Without realizing it, his anger had
melted away and all he felt was a deep loneliness.

Intrigued by the festive atmosphere, Asmodeus decided
to take a tour of the outside perimeter of the celebration
site, remaining well concealed in the grasses. He paused and

contemplated each site of games, sporting events, foods, and classes of all sorts. All were now mostly deserted, as more and more families were tired and heading for home. There was one last place where something was still going on. A large rock sign read, "Miss Hissy's Story Time." A huge group of snakes sat pressed together in a tight circle around an older female snake with perfectly groomed scales. Asmodeus jumped back as loud hisses erupted from the crowd. He watched the storyteller lean down towards the front row of excited snakes. Her movements were slow and exaggerated as she spoke. Suddenly she perked up and shouted, "Kukulkan." A hush fell over the audience.

Asmodeus startled and felt unsettled. He didn't know why, but his mind was in turmoil. He had never heard that word before, Kukulkan, but felt it was somehow significant. Out of nowhere, panic began setting in. He felt suffocated despite being in the open air. All the sights and sounds were too much for his brain to absorb. The seclusion and safety of his den called to him; he had to get home. As Asmodeus was turning to leave, he heard the storyteller's voice take on an eerie tone as she ended her story, "That's all for tonight. Beware of the ghosts of Kukulkan and its land that swallows creatures whole. And beware of the giant snake with legs and arms."

Asmodeus became paralyzed at the warning. He numbly stared at the last of the celebrants talking and joking as they left the foothills of Mandihar's mountain. The desire to go home overwhelmed him, but at the same time he couldn't divert his gaze from one snake. It seemed he knew her . . . but that couldn't be. Then he remembered—she was the young snake who had stared at him through the window of his den this morning.

Asmodeus somehow forced himself to function, and in a confused daze he followed the young snake and her family to their home.

CHAPTER 10

GAIA AND LUCIMA'S PLAN

Gaia lay curled up on her grass bed, trying to sleep after returning home from Pharaoh's party. It seemed odd to come home without him, but she knew he would be away with Mandihar for only a short time. Gaia had enjoyed playing all the games at the celebration, and she had even enjoyed story time since Miss Hissy added the tale about Kukulkan. She didn't know whether it was that scary story or all the spider-cream she had eaten that now made her stomach feel queasy. She readjusted her body to get more comfortable, hoping that would help.

Gaia couldn't seem to shake off the sight of Asmodeus's purple eye. She rolled back and forth at the image that seemed branded in her brain. She didn't understand why her mother refused to believe her. Usually, she could tell her mom anything, but lately she seemed more closed off.

Her churning stomach was not subsiding, so Gaia decided

to go outside for some fresh air. Loud snoring echoed off the den walls as she passed her parents' room on her way to the exit shaft.

Breathing in the cool night air rejuvenated her body, and slowly her nausea diminished. Gaia looked up in wonder at the stars, her curiosity running wild as she thought of the universe and the amazing secrets it held. She wondered if Asmodeus ever looked up at the beautiful nighttime sky. She knew that sleep was out of reach, so decided to sneak over to Lucima's den.

Lucima crept out of her small bedroom window after hearing Gaia calling quietly from outside.

"Gaia, what are you doing here?"

"I couldn't sleep."

"Well, don't wake my mother. She's still mad that we didn't wait for her at the celebration."

With great excitement, Gaia explained to Lucima what she had seen at Asmodeus's den.

Lucima perked up as the story unfolded.

"We should go over there and spy on him right now," Lucima breathlessly whispered.

Gaia smiled at the thought. "Oh, Lucima, let's do it!"

Immediately upon agreeing with Lucima, Gaia had second thoughts. Her mind was in overdrive tonight. The more she thought of Lucima's proposal, the more she thought that probably nothing would happen and they would end up disappointed. After all, she had been going to her grandparents' den her entire life and this was the first time she had ever seen any movement at Asmodeus's den. He was probably so scared now at her seeing him that he would not venture near the window for another decade.

"I don't know, Lucima. It might turn out to be boring."

"But Gaia, you are so freaked out by his third eye, why wouldn't you want to go see?"

Gaia thought for a minute.

"True . . . true . . ." Suddenly, Gaia had a fabulous idea, better than waiting for old purple-eye Asmodeus. "You want an adventure, Lucima? I mean a real adventure?"

Lucima's dark-brown eyes lit up. "Yes, always! What is it?"

Gaia looked around to make sure no one was listening, even though it was the middle of the night and by now all of Moon Meadow was fast asleep. "Let's go to Kukulkan!"

Lucima's face went blank. Her small jaw dropped open. "Kukulkan? You said Kukulkan?"

A mischievous smile spread over Gaia's face. "Yes . . . Kukulkan!"

Lucima squirmed in the grass. "I don't know, Gaia. Kukulkan is haunted. No one ever goes there! Well, I mean, no one ever returns from there."

Gaia snickered at Lucima's apprehension. "Those are just scary stories, myths." Gaia sounded much more confident than she really felt, but the idea had taken hold of her, and she couldn't back down.

Lucima shook her head back and forth. "I don't think so, Gaia. My parents are terrified of Kukulkan. They always speak of a friend of theirs who was swallowed up by the earth and never returned to his family."

Gaia had heard similar stories, but her curiosity had taken

hold of her, and she couldn't give in to fear. She assumed an air of bravado. "Oh, come on, listen to what you are saying. Swallowed up by the earth? You really believe that stuff?"

"I always thought you believed it too, Gaia. The thought of Kukulkan makes me sick."

Lucima hesitantly said, "OK, Gaia. I will go with you, but I don't like the idea."

Gaia's eyes lit up. "Oh, Lucima, this is going to be something we will never forget!"

The two best friends became engrossed in planning the details of their adventure. After much discussion, they decided they would depart at the time of the next full moon, which was two nights away. They decided to call it a night, wanting to get a good rest before their long trek. They had been so consumed with the thought of going to Kukulkan that they didn't notice a sliver of purple peering through the tall grasses, watching the two young snakes slither excitedly back to their dens.

Just the thought of going to Kukulkan made Gaia's stomach do flip-flops. When she got home, everything was quiet, but she was not ready to sleep, so she slithered up a rock and coiled on it. She felt her body relax instantly as she gazed at the almost-full moon that by now had risen high over the mountains. She closed her eyes and lifted her face to the heavens. Much to her surprise, it wasn't Kukulkan that came into her mind; it was Kimba. Gaia had seen him from a distance at the celebration, but he was with friends, so she didn't approach him. She thought he had seen her too. Just thinking of him made her feel an excitement she had never felt before.

Gaia's coil tightened instantly, ending her reverie. Out of

the corner of her eye, she had seen a slithering motion in the tall grasses. She panicked, thinking it might be one of Mandihar's cobra security guards, but then realized tonight was a holiday and there were no guards. Gaia put her head as low as she could and tried to quiet her vibrating tail. She watched in terror as the slithering phantom headed right for her den. She gasped and put her head high up in the night air when a snake's head poked out of the grass. Relief rushed over her when she realized who it was.

Kimba didn't notice Gaia sitting on the rock. Quietly, he crept onto the path in front of her. Gaia wondered what Kimba was doing at her home. Something long and thin dangled from his mouth, but a dark shadow kept its identity a mystery. Gaia's curiosity was piqued as she watched Kimba carefully bend over and place the item at her den's entrance. Turning to leave, he jumped back, startled.

"Oh, hi, G-G-Gaia. You s-s-sc-cared me."

Gaia smiled at him, mesmerized by his luminous yellow eyes. "Sorry, I didn't mean to."

An awkward silence filled the air as they both tried to think of what to say. Gaia spoke first. "What are you doing here?"

Kimba shyly replied, "I wanted to g-g-g-give you something."

Gaia strained her neck to see what Kimba had laid down. He slithered to the side, revealing a beautiful white desert lily. Kimba seemed embarrassed, looking down at the ground as he spoke.

"I was on my way h-h-h-home from the f-f-f-festival; I live just down this p-p-p-path."

Gaia's heart pounded with excitement. He was so cute.

Kimba continued. "I d-d-d-didn't think you would be out and wanted to s-s-s-surprise you."

He looked up cautiously at Gaia. She was beaming. "Thank you," she said softly as she slithered down off the rock towards the lily. "I love it."

The two just sat nervously smiling at each other.

"You're welcome, G-G-G-Gaia."

Kimba's beautiful eyes made Gaia melt. He was different from the other boys in her class, physically strong yet gentler and kinder. She had never experienced feelings like this for anyone else.

"S-s-sorry, my stutter gets worse when I'm n-n-nervous."

"Don't worry. I'm nervous too."

They both laughed.

"Well, guess I'll s-s-see you in class."

"Yeah, see you in class."

Kimba slowly started creeping down the path toward his den. Gaia sat watching until he disappeared into the night. She jumped up in the air and did a little twirl before plucking the flower up with her mouth and heading inside. Now, for sure, sleep would evade her.

CHAPTER 11

THE LIST

Miss Hissy brushed her neck scales with the tip of her tail as she sat perched in front of her empty classroom. Her head nodded rhythmically up and down as she seemed to be rehearsing the next day's lesson. Every few minutes she paused, scanned the room, then let out a loud, playful cackle while gently rocking back and forth.

"What is she doing?" Gaia asked Lucima as they coiled on the dirt hill just outside the schoolyard. The two friends loved meeting here on Sundays because it was always vacant. They had a lot to discuss, since last night they had agreed to travel to Kukulkan. Both were giddy over the thought of their adventure and had to talk about it more.

"No idea. Anyway, why is she at school on Sunday?" asked Lucima.

"Who knows." The two best friends continued their whispered conversation, leaving Miss Hissy to her strange antics.

"He what?" Lucima squealed quite loudly.

Gaia tried to hush her but giggled at Lucima's reaction

before she said, "He brought me a beautiful desert lily at my den last night."

"Tell me everything, Gaia. I need details," Lucima said excitedly.

Gaia could still feel the warmth she felt with Kimba as she spoke.

"He—" Gaia stopped midsentence as a loud cackle came from the school. She and Lucima turned to watch Miss Hissy's charade. Her voice had grown louder as she continued speaking to the air. Her mouth seemed to enunciate each word slowly, making large, exaggerated motions. Suddenly she threw her head back in deafening, hysterical laughter.

"What a freak," Gaia said.

"Why do you think she is acting so weird?"

Gaia smirked as she replied, "Maybe it's that time of year . . ."

Lucima scratched her head with her tail.

"You know . . . maybe she is shedding."

Both girls burst out laughing.

"She is something else," Lucima replied as she flung her head back dramatically, batting her eyes at Gaia.

Their laughter became uncontrollable as they rolled on the dirt.

"Oh, darling, how do I look?" Lucima asked in a high-pitched voice, fluffing her neck scales with the tip of her tail.

"Fabulous, of course," gasped Gaia between fits of laughter.

Miss Hissy became quiet suddenly; all her playfulness ceased while her face grew tight. Gaia could see the fear in Miss Hissy's eyes. Their laughter stopped as Gaia pressed up closer to her friend to get a better look.

"Who's in there with Miss Hissy?"

Lucima shrugged. "I don't know."

Gaia straightened her neck as high as she could, squinting her eyes to help bring the distant schoolroom into focus. Slowly a large, thick, muscular body emerged into view. The sun cast a shadow of an enormous cobra hood over Miss Hissy.

Gaia gasped softly. "It's Mandihar!"

Slowly, Mandihar slithered closer to Miss Hissy. Gaia remained pressed to Lucima, watching in complete silence as Miss Hissy bowed down in total submission.

The girls caught a glimpse of the two large fangs hanging from his devilish grin. His mouth moved rapidly.

"What is he saying?" asked Gaia.

"I can't tell. I've never seen Miss Hissy scared before," Lucima replied.

"Come on, follow me," whispered Gaia as she quickly slithered down the dirt hill toward the large desert willow tree that loomed high above the school. Lucima followed her to the leaning, twisted trunk, which provided perfect cover. Neither of them uttered a word as they strained to listen.

Mandihar was bellowing his questions.

"Where is the list?"

Gaia couldn't see what was happening, but Miss Hissy's meek, distant voice made it known she was still bowed forward.

"I am still working on it, sir. I apologize for—"

An irritated Mandihar cut off Miss Hissy midsentence.

"I don't want apologies, Florence. I only want answers."

With eyes that lit up, Gaia mouthed to Lucima, "Florence?"

Both girls rocked back and forth trying to contain their laughter.

"Yes, sir, I will have it to you right away, first thing in the morning."

"I better have it first thing tomorrow or you will pay the price, Florence."

Slight sobbing came from Miss Hissy as she tried to speak, stuttering her words.

"Y-y-es, s-s-s-sir. To-to-tomorrow."

Mandihar's voice lowered ever so slightly.

"I know a few names on it already, like that Coiler girl—or I should say, E6—but I must know *all* the names."

Only the rustle of leaves on the tree above them could be heard as Gaia's eyes almost popped out of her head. Her tail began vibrating, but she quickly gained control and remained still. All she could do was stare at Lucima, too afraid that even a whisper would be heard. Lucima's concerned look made it clear to Gaia that she had not misheard the conversation. *What list and why is my name on it? What have I done?* The deafening silence only accentuated the rising panic setting in.

A few more minutes passed, feeling to Gaia like eternity, before a loud wailing came from inside. Out of the corner of her eye, Gaia saw Mandihar slipping out of the side entrance of the school that led back to his cavern. The two waited a few minutes until he was completely out of sight before making their way back to the hill. Still quiet, Gaia and Lucima looked in at Miss Hissy.

"Gaia, what list was Mandihar talking about?"

Before Gaia could answer, Miss Hissy flopped her pristine

body down hard on the dusty floor and began quivering with each wail. Gaia was overtaken by paranoia; suddenly she did not feel safe.

"Let's get out of here."

Lucima must have picked up on the urgency in Gaia's voice because she said nothing further before turning and following Gaia into the tall grasses.

CHAPTER 12

GAIA AND LUCIMA SET OUT FOR KUKULKAN

The tall grasses along the meandering, grassy banks of the Snake River swayed rhythmically in the cool west wind that was blowing in a much-needed thunderstorm. Their white plumes stood in stark contrast to the grasses' dark-green stems growing in the sandy soil Gaia and Lucima were now gliding over. The sun shone sporadically between the grey clouds, warming the young snakes' backs.

Neither Gaia nor Lucima had spoken much since they left Moon Meadow earlier in the morning, their minds focused on what was to come. They had told their parents they were going on a picnic with their friend and her family and then were going to have a sleepover at their den. They anticipated being home around midday the next day.

They continued to travel along the banks of the Snake River for a long distance. Lucima seemed to be in a heightened state of nervousness; the occasional sound of distant gunfire from a Leg Walker hunting party made her jump, but she continued. Finally, they emerged into the desolate terrain of the protected region of ancient rock formations, lava fields, and a huge rift in the ground. In the distance, they saw the legendary, towering rock known in the snake world as Kukulkan.

Gaia stopped to rest with Lucima following her lead. Their cream-colored bellies rose and fell at a rapid rate while they stared in awe at the height of the rock tower looming over the entire area. Deep vertical grooves cut into the reddish-brown granite and sporadic ledges jutted out from the side of the rock formation. Gaia squinted to see the top ledge, where supposedly HOXD bathed in the moonlight every full moon.

Even from afar, the sight of Kukulkan caused Lucima to become hysterical. "Gaia, I can't do this!"

Gaia turned to look at Lucima, who had thrown herself over a large rock and vomited. She then began to hyperventilate. Between short, gaspy breaths, she screamed. "*I can't do this!*"

Gaia rushed over to her friend and rubbed her head slowly along Lucima's side, trying to soothe her nerves. Soon Lucima's breathing slowed. Gaia looked directly into two terrified eyes.

"Oh, Lucima, I am so sorry. I didn't know you were so scared."

"Oh, Gaia, I wanted to do it for you, but I just can't . . . I just can't."

Gaia rubbed her head on Lucima's. "It's OK, we can go back home."

Lucima shot up and sat completely straight. "No way, Gaia! I will go home by myself, but you must continue."

Gaia sat, bewildered by her friend's reaction. "Really? You want me to keep going?"

"Of course, I do! Just because I am a wimp doesn't mean you have to be."

Simultaneously, they broke into laughter.

"You are so brave, Gaia, something I am not. Please go . . . for both of us!"

"But what about you?"

"Don't worry about me, I will be OK. You go. Hurry!"

Gaia silently nodded her head in agreement. She stretched over to Lucima and rubbed her head one final time.

"Be careful..."

Gaia gave a sly little smile.

"I will."

Gaia turned quickly and began her race to Kukulkan. While she made a mad dash toward the unknown, she called out into the wind.

"This one is for both of us!"

Again, neither of them noticed a purple streak in the reeds by the river.

CHAPTER 13

GAIA AND THE AVENUE OF THE DEAD

Gaia reached the barbwire fence at the perimeter of Kukul-kan. She stopped for a brief second to catch her breath as she took in the immensity of the ancient rock tower. A complexity of emotions coursed through her body: awe, admiration, fear. Never had she dealt with such conflicting feelings. The heat from the late afternoon sun beat on her back as she sat transfixed. Distant chirping intermittently interrupted the silence as she scouted the surrounding barren landscape.

Everything appeared still, almost as though no life existed except a few desert crickets. Doubt began clouding her thoughts. Could it really be that HOXD lived inside that huge rock? If this was true, wouldn't the tower be shaking with each movement of the gargantuan beast? Had she let her imagination get the best of her? Gaia's mind kept replaying the tales her father told, narrowing it down to the ending. An uneasiness gripped her as she listened to the warning: "Only the unwise would attempt to enter Kukulkan, for to access the tower and HOXD, one must travel on the *Avenue of the Dead*."

Now that Lucima was gone, Gaia's confidence dwindled as she began second-guessing all her decisions. Could it be that the true danger was the surrounding landscape and not actually Kukulkan? Was there truth to all the deaths that had supposedly occurred on the Avenue of the Dead? Gaia tried to quell her racing mind to no avail. The mythical gauntlet had somehow transformed into reality, and it was playing with Gaia's mind. She tried sifting through the noise inside her head, searching for a nugget of helpful information. Nothing appeared. Just the replaying that supposedly hundreds of lives had been lost within seconds of going beyond the fence, vanishing into the bowels of the earth. Gaia looked down at the ground. She could have sworn it was starting to move.

Suddenly her mind envisioned a huge, toothless mouth with a fat, floppy tongue opening wide, engulfing her into blackness. She could almost feel the spray from the beefy red muscle as it pushed her down its throat to join the others from years ago. The mere thought forced Gaia's small body into action; she could not sit still any longer. Impulsivity overcame her as she shot under the barbwire fence.

Instantly, the firm ground became boggy, making it almost impossible to move. Gaia frantically swerved her body back and forth to prevent getting stuck. Never in her life had she experienced such odd terrain, and instinct told her to not stop. Small grunts filled the air as Gaia struggled to cross this forbidden land. Several times, her light body became slightly submerged in the wet sand with her head still poking up. Gaia gasped for air as she struggled forward for what seemed like eternity. Exhaustion was setting in.

Just as Gaia's body slowed almost to a standstill, the ground firmed and she was able to gain more traction. Her gasp was one of relief and thankfulness. However, it was short-lived as the more solid ground began to split, causing Gaia to come to a halt.

Deep crevices zigzagged in all directions. Millenia of unshaded, intense sunlight seemed to have created a maze-like terrain, far-reaching in scope. Gaia carefully wiggled over to the nearest cleft in the earth, slowly extending her head over the edge to see what she was dealing with. A few small pebbles toppled over the edge, vanishing into darkness. Gaia never heard them land. She looked back to the dangerously unstable soil she had just crossed, then forward to the maze of crevices.

She slowly picked her way through the maze of tricky fissures, praying she would not slip over the edge. The crevice she was following gradually narrowed, comforting her worried mind as she imagined a huge expanse of solid dirt ahead. Without warning, she was stopped short by an enormous cleft appearing directly in front of her. Her stomach sank at the sight of it running horizontally, connecting to the other two wide fissures on her sides. A low humming sound emitted from it.

"I'm trapped," she said, exasperated.

The sun's rays seared her scales as she headed back to the beginning of the maze. She tried squashing her inner crescendo of alarm as she analyzed the landscape.

I am going to fry to death, she thought to herself.

Every avenue seemed to end with the splitting of the earth. Her mind began playing with her, doubting every thought.

Don't go that way, Gaia, unless you want to die. Gaia yelled at herself, "Stop it!" She looked to the right. *Oh no, don't go that way.*

Gaia sat straight up and yelled, "Shut up!"

Silence.

Gaia snickered at winning the fight, then burst into nervous laughter when she realized she was fighting with herself.

I'm losing it, she thought as her chuckle faded.

She inched over to the edge of the crevice and glanced down into an endless abyss.

"Oh, my Serpens, I don't want to die." She looked up to the bright sky for help. "Please help me," she begged.

"Please . . . anybody . . ."

CHAPTER 14

ASMODEUS UNLEASHES HIS POWER

Asmodeus was trying to decide whether to follow Gaia or Lucima. He was astounded by the sight of Kukulkan and wanted to know more; however, before he could decide, a huge thunderstorm cut loose right above him.

Nostalgia always gripped Asmodeus's soul during stormy weather ever since losing his brother in that horrible accident. But he also felt a strange euphoria—a strange mixture of emotions that always left him feeling confused. It was almost a primal instinct. He had tried many times putting it into words, but it never made sense. The feeling came from so far deep down inside that it scared him.

A small electrical charge coursed through his veins as a bolt of lightning lit up the sky, causing his purple third eye to twitch involuntarily. This strange phenomenon was always accompanied by a short-lived burst of energy. Now, a huge flash of lightning lit up almost the whole of Kukulkan, causing

Asmodeus to go into a state of mania. Before the thunder had time to boom, he had already slithered from beneath the grasses in which he was hiding and out into the raging deluge.

He slithered quickly as the pelting rain hammered him. His two side eyes focused straight ahead as his purple eye looked upward to the flashing sky. The constant electrical show that was unfolding stimulated the purple eye, filling it with an energy that had to be released. Asmodeus came to a large boulder and found partial shelter beneath a tree. There he coiled himself into an upright position with his head extended backward, opening his third eye fully to the power of the universe.

The sky let out another electrical discharge directly into Asmodeus's soul, forcing his body a few inches off the ground, briefly hovering in midair before falling back down. Immediately upon landing, he extended his neck fully as he locked his gaze onto the nearby boulder. Every muscle rippled from the power building inside his cells as his third eyelid raised fully, revealing the entire spasming purple eye. Small bursts of yellow light shot out of the purple eye as its energy transferred to the boulder, lifting it slowly into the wet air. Asmodeus gripped his tail to the ground with all his might as the boulder continued its ascent to the heavens. Images of his brother floated in and out of his mind as he sat convulsing from the energy overload. The rock shifted a few feet to the side as it remained suspended high above. Asmodeus's insides shuddered one final time before the rock fell straight down, crashing into the mud, splattering his face.

Asmodeus collapsed under the tree, his shaking body gradually becoming still as his breathing slowed. The storm continued east in its destined path as his purple eye fluttered a few times before shutting completely as he fell into this nature-induced hypnotic state, which always included dreams he never understood—and that terrified him.

Now as he lay in a vulnerable state close to the entrance to ancient Kukulkan, his body twitched involuntarily, and his entire body intermittently stretched out rigidly toward the tower, as if reaching for something. In a swirling, shifting fog he could see the shadowy image of a huge snake opening a door into a blindingly bright light that drew Asmodeus toward it. He tried to slither but couldn't. He couldn't see what held him back but only heard cruel laughter. Asmodeus struggled and struggled to move toward the slowly closing door, but he couldn't move, and the door closed, leaving him alone in the darkness.

Asmodeus awakened alone and confused by one of his unrelenting dreams. Somehow this dream had been different from the others, only he couldn't say exactly how. The storm had passed, and the immensity of Kukulkan was now accentuated by the full moon. Both Gaia and Lucima were gone. He moved nervously in circles, trying to decide whether to go home or continue his trek to Kukulkan. Before he made a conscious decision, instinct took over and turned his body in the direction of the looming rock tower. Swiftly, he put his head down and, with his flicking tongue, followed Gaia's scent.

CHAPTER 15

LUCIMA FINDS HER WAY HOME

Lucima's hysteria almost recurred as she struggled to find her way back to Moon Meadow. As the youngest snake in her family, she was never allowed to venture far from her family den without a parent or older snake accompanying her. Consequently, she always followed and never developed an independent sense of direction or knowledge of terrain and how reading its signs was vital in choosing the right paths and avoiding dangerous ones.

Shortly after Gaia headed north for Kukulkan and Lucima turned south, the thunderstorm moved directly in Lucima's path. She became disoriented by the deafening bursts of thunder that immediately followed huge, bright flashes of lightning and suddenly found herself lying tangled in a thorny bush. No matter which way she moved, the sharp spikes tore at her scales. She had no idea where she was and felt so stupid for not staying with Gaia, but the thought of that seemed almost worse than where she was now.

The storm was lessening as it moved quickly to the northeast. Lucima moaned with every attempt at freeing herself. An unusual sound caught her attention. At first she thought it was the rain getting heavier again, but after listening more closely she realized it wasn't. This noise was loud, gurgling, running water . . . the river. Lucima hadn't even realized she had veered away from it. Hope overcame her as she twisted every way she could to avoid the thorns, but it wasn't possible. Finally, she made one swift slither to get the pain over with. The bush was merciless, stabbing Lucima multiple times before releasing her from its grip. Lucima looked down at her punctured body but was relieved the cuts were not deep and were oozing blood, not pouring. She lay panting on the sand and let the light rain cleanse her wounds. Then she carefully headed toward the river to follow it home.

Fatigue set in as Lucima reached the final path to her den. As she approached, she saw her mother nervously slithering back and forth in front of the den's entry. Off to the side sat her father, coiled like a sentry.

Her mother's praying floated through the air: "Oh Holy Serpens, help us."

Lucima stopped as she met her father's eyes. Immediately he stretched out into a full slither toward her, with her mother following his lead.

The worry in her mother's eyes intensified as she got closer.

All three touched heads for a minute in silence. Slowly, her parents assisted Lucima into the den and laid her down on a bed of soft grasses.

"What happened, Lucima? Where have you been?" her mother asked in a tremulous voice.

Lucima was so tired. "Well, we went on a picnic and then . . ."

"Stop right there," her father said in a loud, angry tone. "We know that's a lie."

Lucima avoided eye contact with her parents. She knew she couldn't tell them about Kukulkan, and she would never, ever betray Gaia.

"OK . . . I just wanted to feel what it's like to be independent and to think and do for myself. So I decided to go for a slither through the woods on my own. I got lost."

"Oh, Lucima," her mother whispered.

Lucima continued, "And I got tangled up in a thorny bush. It took me a long time to get out . . . and I have a lot of sores . . . that hurt a lot!" She readjusted herself in bed, "I just need some sleep, Mom."

Her mother had a horrified look on her face and started to ask, "What about independence and free—" but Lucima's dad stopped her.

"Let her rest tonight," he said, "but tomorrow she will have a lot to answer for."

Lucima watched the tails of her parents slither towards the living room. Before they were out of view, she dozed off.

The lunch Mandihar had given Pharaoh to help him relax was very effective. The old wizard estimated that Pharaoh would sleep at least a few more hours. He had some work to catch up on and so headed for his office, which was just off the common area where Pharaoh slept.

Mandihar loved his office and regretted he didn't have more time to spend there. It was filled with a rare collection of ancient clay figurines that were apparently thousands of years old. They depicted bizarre animals and scenes and interactions between snakes and monsters. Mandihar loved to imagine the possibilities. He glided over to his favorite mat and was just getting settled when one of the office-help garters—he never bothered to learn their individual names and just called them all "girl"—interrupted his fantasies to tell him there was someone to see him.

"Who is it?" he said brusquely. "I'm not expecting anyone."

"It's a female garter and her daughter, Lucima. She said it is very important."

"Ah, yes," Mandihar said to himself. "I thought Lucima learned her lesson last time." More loudly, he said, "Seat them in the common area, away from Pharaoh. Don't worry about him, he's still resting."

A group of mothers from Moon Meadow had recently started a group called Mandihar's Daughters of Serpens, an early-interventionist group to keep young females safe from any deviant thoughts, ideas, or harmful behaviors, always in keeping with Mandihar's *Guidance Manual for Young Snake Minds*. Lucima's father was going to start a partner group, Sons of Serpens. Mandihar thought they were a wonderful snake couple with obedient, compliant young snakes who would one day make strong, dogmatic leaders of their community.

"Girl" showed Lucima and her mother to the far end of the central cavern where Mandihar was already seated on his elevated mat. When in front of him, Lucima's mom lifted her head as high as possible and then forcefully thrust it to the floor in an act of abject submission. Lucima lifted her head about an inch off the floor and lowered it carefully. This did not escape Mandihar's notice, and he stared menacingly at her. They then coiled on their assigned mats.

"Grand Wizard," her mother began after lifting her head from the floor. "I am sorry to bother you, especially during an initiation, but I—perhaps I should say *we*—have a problem of high urgency. As you teach us in your manual, chapter 3, verse 16, a misguided idea must be addressed when still small, or it will become very dangerous."

Mandihar silently nodded with a philosophical air.

She went on to tell how Lucima said she had gone off by herself for a journey through the woods and lost her way and ended up in a thorny bush, which injured her and caused her much pain.

Mandihar interrupted, seeming somewhat irritated at this minor incident. "Well, Lucima, have you learned your lesson? That you always need someone to look out for your welfare. Look at the suffering that mistake cost you."

Before Lucima could answer, her mother cut in, once again garnering another irritated look from Mandihar.

"That isn't the worst of it," her mother said excitedly. "When my husband and I asked her why she did what she did, she said—and I quote—'I just wanted to know what it felt like to be independent and to think and do for myself.'"

Instantly, Mandihar's entire demeanor changed. His face darkened with anger and his body twisted on his mat. This upstart had the nerve to challenge and disobey every rule he had put down in his guidance manual.

"That is very serious. That is very dangerous," he hissed loudly. "That is a rebel in the making. That cannot be overlooked and must be eradicated. You must be admitted to the Rehabilitation Center immediately."

Mandihar delivered his sentence for Lucima in short, staccato outbursts. No questions were tolerated. It was final, without Lucima speaking a word.

Lucima's mother looked taken aback, but offered no defense.

"Someday, Lucima," she said nervously, "you'll know this was done out of love and for your benefit."

Mandihar could tell his words were sinking in with Lucima by her silence. He sat back and enjoyed the moment. "And always remember," Mandihar said, "it's up to you how long this will last. Once you are ready to throw yourself down before the whole community—and me, of course—and beg forgiveness for your evil and misguided thoughts and promise to never have them again, then you will be forgiven and welcomed back into the fold. If you don't . . ."

Mandihar remembered the last time Lucima was here for a minor incident. She had said a disrespectful word to Miss Hissy. He had been lenient that time and only gave her one week of detention. This time though, he was going to make an example of her. He watched Lucima slither away from her mother, not uttering a word. Her eyes cold and angry. An inner warmth spread through him.

Then, an old cobra slithered with great difficulty into the room. He bowed before Mandihar, who pointed with his tail to Lucima and gave a familiar order. "That is the one right there."

Lucima fell in line behind the ancient snake. Mandihar watched as the two disappeared into the dark tunnel, the thick rock walls punctuated now and then by a small opening to the daylight. He had a satisfied look as they disappeared into the rehabilitation center.

Mandihar called "Girl" to escort Lucima's mother outside. The three of them slithered the length of the central cavern to the far end where Pharaoh was just waking up. The Grand Wizard watched as his initiate's eyes lit up with confusion at the sight of Lucima's mother gliding by.

CHAPTER 16

GAIA MEETS HOXD

Gaia was hysterical as she slowly slithered to the base of the tower, laughing, moaning, laughing again, shaking uncontrollably. A miraculous rescue from the Avenue of the Dead had not come, so she had to find her own way. Maybe it was Serpens who guided her along the path she chose where she truly believed she would die. Whoever or whatever power it was, here she was at the base of Kukulkan.

After earlier assessing her situation in the maze of crevices, she saw two huge, deep openings in the earth with a very narrow strip of solid land separating them, which led to solid ground beyond—a strip no wider than Gaia's small body. One slithering mistake on either side, and she would be gone, just another victim of the Avenue of the Dead.

She didn't remember starting on her way. Her first flashback was creeping along and repeating over and over, "Don't look down! Don't look down!"

But she did. She looked and couldn't stop herself.

Not far below was the gaping jaw of a snake that looked

like it was grinning. A small lizard crawled out of its eye. Gaia almost jumped back, almost slipping.

"Keep going! Look straight ahead!" she shrieked into the silent, unconcerned desert air, and inch by inch she kept moving.

Then something grabbed her tail. She stopped instantly before she was pulled down into the chasm below. Gaia was so terrified; she immediately went into survival mode. Very slowly, she swiveled her head, dreading the sight of what had her in its grasp. Her tail had caught on a branch that was sticking out of the crevice. In what seemed to be eternity, she was able to get it free and make it to safety.

She lay for a long time at the base of Kukulkan, looking up at the rock tower looming over her, and soon she was planning how to get to the top.

Finally, after what seemed like ages, Gaia reached the top of Kukulkan. With the utmost trepidation, she eased her little head slowly up and over the top ledge to make certain she was alone. A huge area of smooth granite sprawled out over the expansive rooftop, which had large pink granite boulders bordering the perimeter. She headed over to a small crevice that lay under a ledge of rock on the other side. Darkness was setting in as she wedged herself into the tight crack and patiently waited for the sun to kiss the sky goodbye. The lingering warmth of the light's beams, along with the compression of the small space, made Gaia languid. Sleep soon overtook her small body.

Loud footsteps snapped Gaia out of her slumber. At first, she thought it was thunder, but looking up at the brightly shining stars, she knew it was something else. The towering ledge of Kukulkan shook slightly, the ground beneath her thumping.

"What have I done?" she mumbled to herself.

Gaia tried taking a deep breath to calm herself, but the restrictive space didn't allow it. Panic set in as she searched for an escape route. She forced herself to remain still despite her instinctual drive to flee for the stairs. There was no turning back. She immediately began rubbing her head on the side of the rock to help ease her mounting anxiety, just as a huge form emerged from the inner stairwell.

Gaia's chest rose and fell rapidly as her tail vibrated uncontrollably at the sight of the enormous creature standing before her. She gulped at the enormous snake standing on two legs with arms dangling at his sides. She wanted to leap up and scream at the top of her lungs, "HOXD is real! He is real!"

But instead, she sat paralyzed.

Gaia observed carefully as HOXD clumsily lumbered over the rooftop, taking in every detail as the warm night breeze tickled her back. The full moon cast a spotlight on the perfect circle of elevated rock that was placed in the middle of the ledge. The muted light of the twinkling stars danced around the moonlight's pronounced beam.

Gaia's eyes slowly analyzed HOXD's body, starting with his feet. They were covered with huge brown worn leather hiking boots like ones she had seen Leg Walkers wearing. Pharaoh and she had nicknamed them "foot prisons." Pale-green skin with sparse patches of tiny black hairs over solid muscle extended out of each boot. Her eyes scrolled up the smooth skin until it abruptly morphed into a combination of dark-green and brown scales, extending all the way up to his thick neck, then following down his arms. Perched atop his massive neck was a perfectly shaped triangular head with immense teeth. Gaia's head snapped back slightly as the moonlight caught the edge of HOXD's backward-curving teeth, accentuating their sharpness. Gaia's heart skipped a beat.

Gaia followed the scales up his long snout and almost passed out at the sight. Smack in the middle of his brown eyes was a third eye. It was deep purple just like Asmodeus's, with the same crusty eyelid. She shook her head in disbelief as her stomach somersaulted. The mysterious presence almost put a spell on Gaia; she was mesmerized.

HOXD sat down on the edge of the elevated circular rock and kicked off his heavy boots, freeing his tired, achy feet. He wiggled his large toes, trying to loosen them after being squished in his boots all day. A loud moan carried over the rock as he swung his legs up onto the slab and lowered his head. Gaia gasped as the purple eye drifted by her. At the exact second it passed her, it blinked. A shudder rippled through Gaia as she lost control of her bladder. A small yellow stream pooled next to her body.

Gaia's breathing became erratic as HOXD sprawled his gigantic body over the elevated rock. His eyes fixed on the full moon as he lay perfectly straight. A soft, slow chanting emerged from his mouth, at first almost a whisper. Gaia strained to hear what he was saying. HOXD tilted his head far back, exposing his thick, powerful neck, and saying a heartfelt prayer.

"Oh energy of the universe
Make me whole
A part of all living things
All that is breathing
All energy."

Gaia strained her tiny head back as far as the crevice allowed, trying to gain the same perspective of the sky as HOXD. Bright white light blinded her for a second, and she vigorously shook her head to regain her focus. HOXD continued to pray.

"Send us light out of darkness
Order out of chaos
My soul is open to you."

Gaia felt an energy shift in the air as she became aware of an unexplainable presence. Quickly she looked behind her, terrified that something evil was lurking, but only the dusty rock wall stood there. Even though she couldn't see anything, she knew she and HOXD were not alone. Shivers ran up her scales at the sight of the moon's silvery rays illuminating HOXD's features. His smooth skin and scales' wide spectrum of colors seemed magical. His chanting began to slow and soften to barely a whisper.

The bright sky flickered a few times and then turned black. Before Gaia could react, the full moon regained its glow and, together with the stars, took control of the nighttime sky.

The night fell silent as HOXD's chanting ended. Within a few minutes, heavy breathing filled the air. Gaia remained perfectly still, afraid that the slightest disruption would wake him. Watching his slow, deep breathing—along with the fresh air—had a hypnotic effect on Gaia. Every rise and fall of his chest put her one step closer to an inescapable trance. She fought the urge to sleep, but eventually her body gave in, loosening its tight coil and letting her mind fall into another dimension.

CHAPTER 17

MIND MELD

The golden fingers of the rising sun probed the cool rock ledge where Gaia sat staring out of her hiding spot, still groggy from last night's fitful sleep. It took her a minute to remember why she was smushed in a tiny crevice on the rooftop of Kukulkan; however, seeing HOXD sleeping in front of her quickly brought her up to speed. The bright, emerging rays of sunlight crept over Gaia's face, helping quiet the shiver in her body. She tilted her head back, welcoming the soothing effect. Her muscles relaxed somewhat as she nervously awaited HOXD's awakening.

HOXD's thunderous groan as he awoke snapped Gaia into hyperawareness. She watched his brown-and-green scales flatten and meld into an unusual color as he stretched his lengthy body. He appeared weary, maybe from sleeping so soundly under the magical moon. Slowly, he looked down at his legs, seemingly pleased that they were beginning once again to regain their vibrant green color and suppleness.

HOXD smiled to himself as he swung his reenergized legs over the edge of the rock circle and sat upright for a few minutes, soaking in the sun's warmth. He glanced around the rooftop, but suddenly his two deep-brown eyes halted at the sight of a tiny green head with two small mocha eyes staring at him from a tiny crevice in the rock ledge across from him. His purple third eye blinked slowly as it adjusted its focus on Gaia.

Gaia couldn't break her gaze with his third eye, but she finally lowered her head, even though she knew it was too late. She had no control over her wildly vibrating tail.

HOXD sized up the tiny snake in front of him. She appeared terrified and alone. He quickly surveyed his surroundings, scanning every inch of the ledge, and was soon convinced she was alone. His gaze returned to Gaia. Her small body was no longer shaking. Instead, she was completely still—almost frozen. Gaia had gone into shock.

He watched Gaia's thin body lay motionless, her eyes wide open, her breathing deep and slow. He hadn't intended to instill such terror in her; however, he understood how his size might be overwhelming to such a small, delicate snake. HOXD's mouth spread into a wide smile as he watched her sleep. All his ancient instincts told him she was not a threat, but he knew she couldn't stay. It would be a serious security breach if she were to learn any more about Kukulkan. He knew in his heart she had to be removed. He surveyed his surroundings one last time to ensure Gaia was alone. Once he felt certain no other snake was hidden in the rocks, he did what he knew he had to do.

HOXD positioned himself directly across from Gaia. His purple third eye stared up at the sky, drawing down energy from the universe in his people's ritual that was as old as time itself. His two normal eyes peered directly at Gaia. A large gust of wind blew the loose sand up into the air, briefly blurring HOXD's vision. He calmly waited as the air cleared. His purple eye continued its quest in the heavens, the half-shade slowly lifting to help increase its scope. The eye strained to attain maximum focus. The atmosphere began changing with each second. Gradually, the wind's occasional gusts became a slow, continuous whirlwind. Dust and small pebbles scattered in the air as the purple eye sank even deeper into its gaze. The air became more agitated, throwing any loose debris into a constant spin. Eerie whining noises permeated HOXD's mind, but nothing could break the concentration of the third eye. Jumbled visions flooded HOXD's mind, images of ancient times when many of his people had this ability and worked together to maximize huge volumes of energy when needed. However, now he was alone.

Kukulkan began to shake slightly as the gusts increased in velocity. The slight shifting of the rock caused Gaia's body to rock gently back and forth as HOXD's normal eyes remained centered on her. The purple eye went into its deepest mode of tapping into the universe. Small pinkish sparkles flashed in the air in front of Gaia. Her tiny body began to move, even though she still lay asleep. The third eye strained even harder, its pupil dilated to full capacity as its lid twitched uncontrollably. Then HOXD's entire body was wracked with a surge of energy he had never experienced before. The heavens were in full force, but more intense than he had ever known. Kukulkan's slight shaking turned into a constant tremble. HOXD's body thrashed around as the rock rattled underneath him. All his eyes remained centered on their missions. The purple eye never lost connection with the sky. A light-orange beam emitted from HOXD's brown eyes to the blue heavens, while the purple eye vibrated with intensity as Gaia's body began to move.

Intense thunder broke the whining of the wind as the energy peaked. Gaia's body slowly swayed side to side before it lifted off the rock. The gale force wind swept under her light body and pushed her even higher in the air. HOXD's body shook more violently than usual. Gaia's body continued to float in the air toward the edge of the rock. HOXD stepped behind her as she moved, hovering for a few seconds over the rooftop's edge. The purple eye was tiring from the strain. Gaia's body began to slowly descend the side of the enormous rock tower. HOXD hung his head over the edge as she lowered to the ground below. The third eye began to spasm right as Gaia's limp body reached the safety of the dirt at the base of the tower. Simultaneously, HOXD's body and the atmosphere became still. The two brown eyes returned their line of sight to Kukulkan. The purple eye relaxed as the eyelid returned to its drooping position. The small rosy speckles emitting from the third eye vanished. The purple eye jerked uncontrollably a few times before falling completely still. HOXD collapsed at the side of the ledge.

The day went grey as the sun hid behind a large passing cloud.

Asmodeus slowly awakened on the warm but barren sand of the huge crater in which stood, not far from him, the Tower of Kukulkan. He was bewildered as to how he got there; the last thing he remembered was coiling in the reed grasses on the edge of the bank now above him before it dropped sharply into the crater. He felt the total exhaustion and confusion he experienced following a thunderstorm, but he had no recall of the usual build-up of intense energy. He slowly lifted his face to the heavens as a brightly shining sun emerged from behind a large passing cloud.

He tried to clear his mind. Slowly, the confused images faded out and he recalled his entry into the cursed land surrounding Kukulkan. He remembered following that young garter to the base of the tower. He watched her disappear as she slithered up the very steep steps, and then recalled feeling overwhelmed by a vague, mysterious familiarity.

More details began emerging in his mind: the growing darkness, the unfamiliar terrain, the rising of the full moon. Now he recalled choosing for his refuge a dense patch of grasses and reeds on the edge of the big bank that dropped off to the crater below.

Asmodeus recalled feeling the presence of his brother. He felt a strange certainty that his brother's spirit was present.

"We'll stay here for a few days, brother," Asmodeus remembered shouting into the empty night that was descending on Kukulkan. "Maybe we'll find a clue to who we are."

Asmodeus couldn't shake the feeling that his brother had heard him and agreed. Never had he felt such a real connection to him, despite missing him every day.

The memory of exhaustion and coiling up to sleep came to Asmodeus as he put his head back as far as possible to see the top of the tower. He could make out the ledge at the top, but barely. Then he recalled that he fell asleep but startled, which made his purple eye pulsate for no apparent reason. This occurred on and off throughout the night, and Asmodeus now understood why he awoke this morning weary and agitated.

Suddenly, Asmodeus shuddered. His purple eye popped wide open, unprotected by the usual half-shade, and began pulsating uncontrollably. The power surge was extreme, unlike anything he had ever experienced. The energy kept building, but he was unable to expel it. He remembered trying to slither away, but he was unable to move. Terror gripped him as he thought he might explode.

The last event became vivid in his mind. He saw a bright-blue, pulsating beam of intense light that seemed to hiss and crackle, almost like it was alive, emitting from his third eye up toward the top of the tower. He felt the same terror now as when it happened. He remembered seeing the blue beam connecting to the eye of a very large figure. The darkness made it hard to see any details beyond the glowing purple eye. Asmodeus vibrated as he recalled seeing a small form floating down to the ground. Right before losing consciousness, an explosive burst of energy coursed through the beam, blowing him over the edge of the cliff.

.

CHAPTER 18

BACK AT MANDIHAR'S CAVE

"*The world has not always been as we know it today.*" Mandihar began reading after returning to the main room and coiling opposite Pharaoh as he spoke. Pharaoh was still a little groggy and on edge from the unnerving screams he had heard. He was still wondering why Lucima's mother had snubbed him as she left the cavern. The full moon had replaced the sun in the roof openings and now lent an eerie glow to the cavern. Mandihar sensed Pharaoh's apprehension and offered him a tree frog to try.

While he waited for it to take effect, Mandihar scanned the golden tablet in front of him, admiring the sacred knowledge carved into it. His chest swelled with pride. Gradually, Pharaoh's posture loosened and his eyes drooped. Mandihar smiled. As he watched his young initiate feel the effects of the tree frog, he thought, *With you by my side, Pharaoh, I will keep all the young males in line.*

He gently stroked the tablet. Mandihar caught Pharaoh staring at him and quickly regained his composure. "Like I was saying, HOXD's people were different and had powers no one else could understand."

For once Pharaoh didn't scoff at the mention of HOXD. Mandihar resumed reading from the secret text.

"Serpents were among the most ancient creatures that are known today. And snakes are the descendants of those huge serpents. As I said before, some of those snakes had two legs and small arms; they walked upright."

Mandihar paused as the female garter slid in to drop off another tray of snacks and began again when she left.

"Those times were mysterious. Many life forms came into being . . . very different life forms, some called Snake People, who had powers no one else understood. Eventually, they spread all over the ancient world, teaching people about the heavens and the Earth and the interactive power of nature . . . the human Leg Walkers came much later . . . wars broke out. Snake People disappeared from the face of the Earth along with their knowledge.

"Listen very carefully to this next part," Mandihar said, but only after giving Pharaoh a threatening stare.

Pharaoh sat up straighter.

"From ancient, incised clay tablets to modern geological discoveries, we know the Snake People knew how to reproduce living creatures from combinations of already existing

life forms. This lost ancient wisdom included a blueprint for snakes with limbs using small energy switches that controlled whether snakes had legs and arms. Turn the switch on: snakes grow legs and arms. Turn the switch off: snakes did not grow legs or arms. Long ago, somehow that switch was turned off permanently."

Mandihar pushed the tablet to the side and grabbed the next one. Pharaoh interrupted. "What do you mean 'blueprint'?"

Mandihar smiled at Pharaoh's interest.

"It's a plan showing how something works," Mandihar said.

"Aaaahhhh," Pharaoh answered slowly.

Mandihar found his place on the new tablet.

"In later times, it was told that snakes lost their legs as punishment for being evil, and that they must forever crawl on their bellies. Through many thousands of years of teaching and repeating this, the concept of all serpents as evil became imprinted in the psyches of other species, especially Leg Walkers, who still see snakes as frightening and loathsome."

Pharaoh leaned forward as Mandihar reached for the last tablet. It was slightly larger than the others and glistened in the moonlight. Only one sentence was inscribed on it.

"HOXD: Immortal keeper of ancient wisdom at Kukulkan."

Mandihar looked up from reading. "Did you get that? HOXD has this information at Kukulkan . . . and I am going to find it. I must find it!"

It scared Pharaoh that he was beginning to see Mandihar's point of view, but the possibility of gaining power also excited him.

"Wait, what about the Leg Walkers? Shouldn't we go after them?" he asked.

Mandihar smirked at the thought of Pharaoh joining his side. "Oh, the Leg Walkers don't have the ancient wisdom. In fact, they have been searching for it for thousands of years. First, we must deal with HOXD. We'll deal with the Leg Walkers another day."

Pharaoh smiled at the thought of one day having revenge on the Leg Walkers. Now his mind churned with anticipation. "But why the emphasis on legs and arms? You have such deadly venom that everybody is terrified of you, even Leg Walkers."

Mandihar set aside the tablets and came down from his mat. He began answering calmly. "Even though we have that, we are really quite helpless in most situations against Leg Walkers."

Then his speech quickened as he began slithering in small circles in front of Pharaoh.

"It's very limiting to have to get around crawling on your belly." Mandihar's voice grew louder. "And it's humiliating! We must have access to HOXD's information!"

Pharaoh was stunned at the intense passion of Mandihar's words. He was unsure of how to answer so decided to remain silent.

Mandihar looked around the room as he paused, trying to control his rising anger. A tall piece of pottery standing next to his head on a low rock shelf caught his attention. It was a sculpture of a tall, thin woman with a serpent head. A sliver of moonlight accentuated her reptilian facial features. In the middle of the shelf lay a rock tablet. On the other end of the shelf sat a sculpture of a rearing cobra head with its hood extended. It was made of solid gold, which shone brightly in the soft light. It was the old wizard's most cherished possession, given to him long ago by his king cobra father, member of a royal family.

Mandihar swelled with a feeling of power just thinking of his lineage; however, his eyes became fierce with the realization that he needed one more thing before he could realize his dream of absolute power. He gave in to the rising rage as he looked down disgustedly at his limbless body and then winced at the sight of Pharaoh's. The thought of his inability to grow legs and arms like HOXD unhinged him. He began ranting under his breath and then shouted maniacally.

"You just wait, Pharaoh. You just wait. I am going to find out the secrets at Kukulkan, and you are going to help me. Yes, I will." Mandihar's eyes narrowed as he ranted. Small drops of spit sprayed out of the corners of his mouth with each emphasized word. His irritation turned into a full frenzy. He slithered with a vacant stare toward one of the back rooms, leaving alone a speechless Pharaoh.

Mandihar slithered down one of the narrow tunnels leading from his cavern into the deep recesses of the mountain, this tunnel suddenly widening into another huge cavern that was almost completely open to the sky. It was filled with an enormous number of plants that flourished in an almost tropical atmosphere. Mandihar always felt better here. The warmth almost immediately had a calming effect on him upon entering. He sat loosely coiled with his face turned up to the sun.

Mandihar didn't know how long he sat there before he sensed Pharaoh sitting next to him. He turned quickly to face him.

"How long have you been here?" he asked abruptly.

"Not long," Pharaoh said, still feeling very relaxed. "I didn't want to interrupt you."

Mandihar remained silent, not knowing how much Pharaoh remembered of his earlier outburst.

"What is this place?" Pharaoh asked, looking around. "It's beautiful . . . and peaceful."

"I would just call it a big garden where we study plants to see how nature works."

"Who is we?" Pharaoh asked.

"I work with other cobras who live in the surrounding area . . . not in Moon Meadow. We study different plants. Some offer relaxation, some heal, and some kill. In fact, sometimes a plant can both heal and kill. It is just a matter of dosage," Mandihar said looking off into the distance. "We still have so much to learn."

"Do any garters work with you?" Pharaoh asked.

Mandihar stared very directly into Pharaoh's eyes.

"Sometimes," he said.

Pharaoh's mind flashed to his old classmate he had seen in the garden outside. He knew it wouldn't be wise to ask more questions, so the wizard and the initiate sat together in silence, with faces turned to the sun. Then Mandihar led Pharaoh back down the tunnel into the main cavern.

"There is so much to learn," Mandihar said, speaking now in an almost affectionate way.

Pharaoh was listening carefully.

A loud cry pierced the air, causing Mandihar to stop midsentence. Pharaoh turned his head toward the long tunnel leading to the other cavern just as another shrill scream penetrated his small body. He quickly turned to Mandihar in a panic. The wizard sat completely still, unaffected by the anguished sounds echoing in the cavern. His eyes appeared to be colder than ever. Pharaoh shuddered as a loud clanking noise erupted. The air went silent. The cries ended as abruptly as they had started.

Mandihar kept his eyes fixed on Pharaoh's. He drew in a deep breath as he flexed his hood and leaned in so close that Pharaoh felt his hot breath on his face. Mandihar paused for a few seconds, staring directly into Pharaoh's eyes.

"I must have that blueprint," he hissed. "Think of it, Pharaoh. Think of what we could be again. The power . . . oh, the power. No longer will we slither on the ground. And you can be part of that!"

Pharaoh was stunned, but Mandihar's words resonated with him. Even though Mandihar intimidated him, it was exhilarating.

Mandihar backed away.

"I know this is a lot for you to take in," he again said in a soft, fatherly way. "Here, take this toad. It will help you relax, and then we can talk more when you feel up to it.

Pharaoh put up no fight, took a bite of the toad, and slipped into oblivion.

Mandihar returned to his elevated position and waited until he was certain that Pharaoh was no longer coherent. Then he began chanting one sentence—slowly and with great emotion—that he would continue repeating until Pharaoh regained full consciousness.

"We must kill HOXD!"

CHAPTER 19

GAIA HEADS HOME

Asmodeus was still lying in the dirt and sand at the bottom of the crater trying to figure out how he was blown off the cliff. Next to him, a small lizard scuttled by and burrowed right below the surface of the dirt, leaving only his nostrils and eyes to be seen. Watching this made Asmodeus realize how vulnerable he was out in the open. Quickly, he slither-hopped up the side of the cliff to the patch of tall grasses in which he had sought refuge. Gently, he separated the green blades and peeked out below.

Gaia's body slowly shifted back and forth at the base of the tower as she awoke from her state of shock. She snapped straight up, darting her head in every direction to see if anyone else was there. Off in the distance, a large tumbleweed blew over the cracked sand. Her insides began shaking at the memory of HOXD; she jumped as a loud screech pierced the air from above. A red-tailed hawk majestically flew by. She quickly sought cover behind a small rock at the base of Kukulkan. Her heart was beating so fast she felt it might fly out of her mouth.

"Calm down, Gaia, calm down," she whispered to herself.

A few more chilling squawks rang high above before the bird was out of sight. Then the ground started to vibrate slightly. Gaia looked like she might be on the verge of a nervous breakdown. Her sides shuddered as small gasps came from her tiny mouth.

Asmodeus watched the little snake below hiding behind the rock. She appeared terrified. Her frantic movements did not fit in with the calm environment, warm sun, and gentle breeze. He empathized with her; he knew how it felt to be amidst the unknown. He wondered what could make her so scared as he looked up the looming side of Kukulkan. Somehow Asmodeus instinctively knew this rock formation had answers, but to what, he did not know.

Gaia appeared faint as she looked down at the ground. A small space opened where the sand met the base of Kukulkan. She held her breath at the daunting sight. Kukulkan did not stop at ground level but instead descended into the dark depths of the earth for a great distance, perhaps greater than that of the tower above. The ground resumed its low grumble, causing loose pieces of sand and stone to plummet into the black void, with no resounding echo of having landed.

A quick thrust of the ground jolted Gaia, causing her to lose her balance and hit her head on the unforgiving dirt. The earth went still for a brief second before returning to its slow, dull vibration. Asmodeus saw Gaia start to hyperventilate, probably at the thought of having to cross the Avenue of the Dead. She gathered her composure and decided on a new way: through the reeds above the crater, then circling far around the tower and finding the river, which she could then follow home. It would take her much longer with no path to follow, but she didn't seem to mind at all.

Asmodeus's two eyes widened as he saw Gaia leave the tower and come toward the field of reeds. She passed him at quite a distance, and he desperately wanted to reach out to her—to comfort her—but he knew he could not. He wanted to follow her home, but an undeniable force kept him still, a force he could not explain but knew he had to obey. His eyes cautiously returned to his vigil at the formidable Kukulkan.

CHAPTER 20

KUKULKAN'S MYSTERIES

"I see you are back in your throne," Meteor joked.

A low chuckle came from HOXD, who sat perched on a massive slab of rock with a deep indentation whose high sides culminated in two carved snake mouths, open and with large fangs. HOXD's hands rested on two carved forked tongues. It was the perfect spot overlooking the lowest level of an immense, very deep cavern beneath Kukulkan. Across the back of the massive rock lay a wooden staff, shaped like a snake, that was thousands of years old. HOXD insisted it remained there untouched; he loved being reminded of the days when he would watch Kukulkan's ancient serpent perform her rituals of healing.

"Looks like another busy day, doesn't it, Meteor?"

Meteor was a garter who had been with HOXD for a very long time. His small, compact, and limbed body exuded strength. Below his left bicep lay a perfectly round piece of a meteor embedded under a layer of scales. Immediately after his birth his parents placed it there in a sacred rite so old that no snake remembered its origin. The chip of meteor was to serve as a lifelong reminder of his origin, which they believed had to do with a mysterious black stone fallen from heaven.

HOXD's eyes drooped as he sat slumped in his chair.

"You OK?" Meteor asked. "You look kinda worn out."

HOXD grinned as he straightened his posture. He was spent, but he didn't want Meteor to know about the rooftop events from this morning.

"Worn out? Nah, just a little tired."

Meteor remained quiet but had a worried frown.

HOXD quickly came up with a reason, hoping Meteor would not ask any more questions. "You know how it is when it's a cloudy night."

Meteor's concern vanished as he sighed with relief. "Aah, yeah. I turned in early last night, so I didn't realize that."

HOXD breathed a sigh of relief.

The two continued in silence, watching the activity below.

A small, irregular hole in the rock far above allowed a thin ray of sunlight through its jagged granite edges. It shone brightly in the upper level, accentuating the cracks running in all directions, ranging from thin, delicate lines to deep, thick crevices. Gradually, the beam turned into a muted grey, and by the time it reached the lowest level, it no longer sparkled off the hundreds of green specks that covered the cavern floor. Shouts of snakes rose above the clanging of tools.

HOXD sat looking down at the workers below, who were his ancient family. Tiny, frail garter snakes moved at what seemed a snail's pace compared with the muscular, compact snakes hauling large rocks on their backs. Some snakes had only arms, some only legs, a few had both, and others had neither. Watching the snakes made HOXD think back to when his experiments first began, and his ancient family was small. He had learned so much through trial and error, which brought on a wave of emotion.

"Every day I sit here it reminds me of how far we have come." Before Meteor could reply, HOXD continued, "And how far we must go."

Meteor nodded in agreement.

"You know, Meteor, I am the last living representative from the very ancient world of the snake."

HOXD continued as he watched a small snake with one arm sweep the floor. "Some would say I am blessed with immortality and all the knowledge that entails, but it comes with a price. Oh yes, definitely a price . . ." His voice trailed off.

HOXD's eyes filled with concern as he receded further into his "throne." An enormous, lifelike feathered serpent swooping down was carved into the wall right above his head.

"You see, before I was born it was only snake lore that spoke of an immortal with a purple third eye. Then I entered the world."

HOXD paused as he reached back for the wooden staff, carefully laying it in his lap, running his fingers over the curve of the snake's head.

"When word of my anomaly circulated through the community, it brought a visit from Kukulkan's revered shaman. According to my parents, she passed out at the very sight of my eye. When she came to, she performed an ancient ritual using this staff to bless my purple eye."

Meteor's eyes watched as HOXD lifted the staff high into the air as he spoke to the heavens. "I spent many years being her understudy. She taught me how life is an intimate part of the universe and everything is connected, somehow tethered to the cosmos."

HOXD pointed the staff at the wall carving. "She claimed to have gotten all of her powers from this winged serpent god."

Both sat in silence for a minute, taking in the detailed etching of the magical deity.

"He was known as Kukulkan. This used to be the temple where the town came to worship him."

Meteor seemed engrossed in the story as HOXD opened up more than usual, allowing new details to emerge.

"The shaman began teaching me how to utilize my powers, but . . ." His head fell forward as he slowly shook it back and forth. "But then the Great War broke out."

HOXD fell silent and stared at the staff almost as though it were alive. He continued in a soft voice. "One day I went to her den and she was gone. Rumor has it the cobras got to her, but no one knows for certain."

Meteor was listening intently.

"But the strangest thing occurred. When I got home, this staff was lying in the entryway of my den. The last time I had spoken to her, she warned me that if an immortal is born without the blessing of the staff, their power can be used for evil."

Those last words hung heavily in the air. Meteor sat patiently. After a few minutes, HOXD replaced the staff behind him and switched his focus to the actions below. "I still feel guilty when I see everyone working so hard for such an uncertain outcome."

Meteor finally spoke, "Come on, HOXD, everyone knows that in order to continue growing there is an element of risk."

HOXD sighed heavily. "I know, I know. But I still feel responsible when things don't turn out as planned."

"Everyone understands. Really, they do."

HOXD felt drained and weary. "I hope so."

The two sat looking around the cavern, taking in the ancient carvings on the back wall. HOXD was reminded of all the pieces of lost and forgotten wisdom by the two serpents with their limbed bodies intertwined and their heads looking up at the moon.

Through plumes of dust filling the air, the two watched a group of young garters below working on Meteor's first solo project. Snakes with both arms and legs pounded granite hammers through the bottom stratum of Kukulkan. HOXD knew Meteor was proud of his first solo project and had been working on it round the clock for weeks.

"I see you have Alset helping you out."

Meteor's eyes lit up. "Sure do."

Alset and Meteor had been inseparable since being snakelets. Alset's arm and leg muscles rippled with each pound of the hammer.

"What exactly do you have them collecting, Meteor?"

"Garnet sand."

"Garnet sand?"

"Yes. You see, if you combine the sand with high-pressure

water, you get a highly abrasive concoction," Meteor smiled, "so powerful it can cut through granite."

"Really? Granite?"

"Indeed."

HOXD sat in admiration of Meteor's findings before saying, "Well, I better go check on the other rooms."

"Do you want company?" asked Meteor.

"Why not, come on."

HOXD hefted his massive body from the throne with Meteor right on his heels. They headed toward the elaborate series of tunnels branching off from the large main room, many leading to small apartments for the inhabitants of Kukulkan. He, however, was heading to the tunnel that contained his research rooms, which held the future of his species.

As they walked together, Meteor asked, "How is it coming with the babies? Any successes?"

HOXD had been working feverishly trying to understand the switch that determined whether snakes had limbs.

"Some success, some failures," HOXD replied as they came to the first room along the elaborate tunnel known as Centralia.

The two entered a room where each wall had a large *E* carved in the middle with mathematical equations surrounding it. The sight of so many numbers and letters sometimes made HOXD feel dizzy.

"It's hard to breathe in here," Meteor said as he inhaled deeply.

HOXD perked up and laughed softly before saying, "The heat definitely sucks the air out of you."

Meteor shielded his eyes with his hand. "Yeah, and the light is blinding."

"Hey, you wanted to come," teased HOXD.

"I know. I'm just not used to it."

HOXD stepped closer to the newborn garters, marveling at one with little bumps on her sides. He pointed to her as he spoke. "Look, she is going to have legs.

HOXD smiled as he looked at the converter that allowed him to control the light and heat in Centralia. It was right below a huge wall carving of an ouroboros, a serpent with its tail in its mouth, continually devouring itself and being reborn. With Meteor's help, he had rigged a solar collector on the pinnacle of Kukulkan Tower, which ultimately fed into this converter.

"So light and heat really can determine whether a baby snake has limbs?" Meteor asked HOXD.

"Possibly. I'm still figuring it out."

HOXD looked at all the newly born snakes wiggling around, once again triggering his concern.

"There is one failure that will always bother me," HOXD began. "It happened long before you were born, but your parents would remember. It was the morning after the day when twenty garter snakes had been born. All the snakes of Kukulkan were excited, including me. When we entered the room, we immediately saw that five young ones were missing."

HOXD paused, looking into the distance before he finished.

"We never found them . . . and we never found who was responsible . . . I think of it every day."

Meteor looked surprised. "You mean there are possibly

five snakes outside of Kukulkan with limbs?"

HOXD shook his head with a worried expression. "Yes, it's possible."

Meteor looked stunned.

"And one more thing, Meteor," HOXD said with alarm in his eyes. "Something I have never told anyone."

Meteor leaned in closer as he listened to HOXD.

"Two of them had a purple third eye."

Meteor's mouth dropped open, but no words came out.

"And they both were gone before I was able to bless them with the staff."

Meteor stood frozen in silence.

HOXD became so full of emotion that he turned and left the room without speaking another word.

CHAPTER 21

GAIA AND PHARAOH BACK AT HOME

"You were where, Gaia?!"
There was more frustration than anger in her father's voice as he shouted at her. Gaia sat before him frazzled. The entirety of her normally polished scales were hidden behind a layer of crusted dirt. That is, except for the small patch atop her head, which was dried and frayed, almost standing straight up into the air. Gaia watched her father's brow furrow as he looked her up and down.

"Kukulkan . . . I didn't think it was such a big deal," Gaia said rather sullenly. She looked around the room at the tired faces of her mother and grandma. Grandpa looked rather stern, as he usually did.

"We were so worried, Gaia," her mother said gently. "Why didn't you tell the truth about where you were going? You know how we feel about lying and breaking trust."

"Would you have let me go if I had told you?" Gaia snapped.

"*No,*" her father practically bellowed. "You know that every young snake is taught that Kukulkan is a forbidden place. You must remember how I hammered that into your heads when I told the story of HOXD on those nights of the moon fires."

"Of course, I remember," Gaia said with sadness in her voice, remembering the peace and security and happiness of those not-so-far-off times. "Your stories always scared me, but I loved them and they made me very curious too. You never said why we couldn't go to Kukulkan, or why it was so dangerous. Why?"

Vasuki broke in on Gaia's question. "It's part of our history that has come down to us for thousands of years," he said. "No snake questions it. It's part of our way of life and everything we believe. In fact, Mandihar does not allow our dens to speak of it in a serious way—only as a scary story for the young snakes who must learn that lesson. Our wizard is very strict about that."

Vasuki shot a quick glance to his father, who gave a meaningful glance in return. It wasn't lost on Gaia, and she pushed harder.

"Do you really mean that none of you have ever gone to Kukulkan?" Gaia asked. "It isn't that far from here."

Her grandma answered quietly. "Females would never go on such a journey alone. And we are never allowed in any discussions about such things." She watched as her mother nodded in agreement.

Then Gaia's grandpa, a snake of few words, chimed in. "I followed the river a few times to where you leave its shore and go into the rocky lands where in the distance you can see the Kukulkan Tower, which I imagine you saw too, Gaia, but I never went any closer. And I never told anybody."

Gaia noticed her dad's demeanor change as he had an amused look on his face.

"You too?" Grandpa asked, surprised.

Vasuki nodded his head. "I went as far as the fence, but I was scared and turned and got out of there as quickly as possible."

"Sooo," Gaia said, "the males can have an adventure, but the females can't. Why?"

"Because it is the law," her mother said in a resigned way, but Gaia didn't believe she meant it. "Mandihar makes the laws for the dens in Moon Valley and guarantees us everything we need to live well—and peace—if we obey. If we disobey, there is punishment that is subtle but harsh." She paused for a long time and then added, "I guess we chose peace and some prosperity."

"Or being controlled," Gaia said softly. Before anyone could offer a challenge, she looked to her dad and grandpa and asked, "Did either of you ever see HOXD?"

The two burst out laughing almost as one.

"HOXD is a fairy-tale ogre. He is not real," Vasuki said with a chuckle. "He is just used to make an impression on young minds. And it has worked for many centuries."

"Well, then, what is so dangerous that we can never go near Kukulkan?" Gaia asked. "It makes no sense."

"Strange things happen there," her grandpa said as he lowered his head to the floor. He would say no more.

"HOXD is real," Gaia stated flatly, her entire small body

trembling as she recalled his third purple eye staring at her.

Gaia's mother and grandma slithered quickly to her sides, pressing close and touching their heads to hers.

"You've had a frightening day," her mother said in a comforting way. "With some rest and lots of Grandma's good food, you'll forget your nightmare and be back to normal soon."

"*No!*" Gaia screamed, startling everyone as she pulled away. "I saw HOXD. He is real!" Gaia's mom and grandma quickly came to her side again. Even though Gaia felt misunderstood, a comfort overtook her as her tightly coiled body pressed between them.

"Where did you see HOXD? Are you sure it was HOXD?"

Gaia looked up, surprised to hear her brother's voice. Pharaoh was sitting in a shadow at the other end of the room. Gaia hadn't realized he was home. He looked how she felt, haggard and confused.

"You can't mistake HOXD for someone else," Gaia said. "And seeing that he doesn't come visiting in Moon Meadow, I went to see him in his Kukulkan Tower."

There was a deathly silence in the room, and everyone just looked at each other.

Finally, her father found his voice and asked quietly, "You went beyond the fence of Kukulkan and actually approached the tower?"

Gaia looked at her father defiantly. "I wanted to see for myself what it was that no one will talk about; and they even lie about it. And no, I didn't approach the tower."

Gaia could almost hear the tension in the room lifting.

"I climbed to the top of the tower, and that is where I saw

HOXD,"

She flinched as a shriek came from her grandma. "Oh, my holy Serpens, you're lucky you're alive!"

Gaia continued with her story about that night of the full moon on Kukulkan Tower to her shocked and horrified family. She finished by telling them that rather than harm or kill her, HOXD saved her life. She wasn't sure how, but he did. The only part of the story she omitted was that of discovering a huge underworld beneath Kukulkan. She wasn't sure why she did that either, but she did. And she most certainly did not mention Lucima. Gaia couldn't wait to see Lucima and tell her all about what she had missed.

As everyone sat in silence, Gaia watched Pharaoh. He appeared sullen and removed. She worried that something had happened while he was at his initiation with Mandihar.

"Why are you home so early, Pharaoh?"

Pharoah stared off into the distance. "Mandihar wanted me to come home for the day and think things over before going back to finish my training."

"Think what things over?" she asked confused.

"You know . . . stuff . . ."

"What—" Gaia's mother interrupted her before she could finish her question.

"Come on, Gaia, leave your brother alone. You know initiates are not supposed to talk about anything . . . let's respect that"

Then her grandma added, "Why don't you get some rest, Gaia? You look like you could use some."

Gaia wanted to continue with her questions, but she was

exhausted. "I think I will go lie down for a while."

Her whole family appeared relieved to get a break from the tension. Everyone except Pharaoh. He still wouldn't make eye contact with Gaia as she slithered towards her room. She would talk to him more when she woke up. Just as Gaia coiled up in her bed, she heard someone arrive at the den entry. A loud, stern voice echoed throughout the den.

"Pharaoh, Mandihar demands your immediate presence in his cavern."

Gaia perked up at the voice's urgency. She wanted to get up and see what was going on, but her fatigued body didn't allow it. She mumbled into her bed of grass, "Tomorrow . . . I will find out tomo . . ." and with that she collapsed into much-needed rest.

CHAPTER 22

COBRA CRUCIBLE

It was pitch-black in the twisting, winding tunnel that led ever deeper into the earth from its starting point at the base of Mandihar's mountain. Just a day earlier, Pharaoh had rejoined Mandihar to learn the next phase of his initiation. The tunnel's entry was well camouflaged in the meadow floor, and no one in the community knew of it. Pharaoh was terrified, and he stayed right on Mandihar's tail as their descent continued for what seemed an eternity. The decline finally leveled off and took a sharp turn to the left. Pharaoh panted as he was forced to keep pace with Mandihar's huge size and strength while they traversed a long distance in silence. Pharaoh thought he saw a small, seemingly insignificant, dot of light far in the distance and watched it anyway to keep his spirit up. Now and then he would also sense a presence behind him, but no one was there. Little by little, though, the dot grew bigger and soon became a bright opening into a scene that was so shocking that Pharaoh felt almost paralyzed; his body instantly coiled more tightly than ever in his life.

Mandihar had summoned Pharaoh to his cavern. After their last initiate session, he sent Pharaoh home to get some rest before he began his training with the army. Now, with his trainee by his side, Mandihar showed off the underbelly of his home.

As far as Pharaoh could see was a massive, deep, cuplike depression in the earth, encircled by towering, sheer, vertical walls of black basalt with razor-sharp edges. A big part of the top of this huge hollow was open to the sky, and at midday the heat of the sun was intense. Pharaoh hung back in the tunnel opening where it was cooler, trying to understand what he was seeing.

Pharaoh's eyes were locked on big pens that contained hundreds of young snakes writhing around with pent-up energy. At intervals around these enclosures were towers of rocks atop which were three huge, musclebound cobras training the young, impressionable troops. Each was equipped with a long whip. Their unhinged shouting resonated in the cavern as they asked, "What do you want?"

The agitated movement stopped instantly and in one strong, loud voice the young cobras replied, "We want limbs!"

"Why do you want limbs?" the three giants shouted again, their combined ravings almost deafening those nearby. Pharaoh winced.

"Limbs bring power and wealth."

Pharaoh felt like he was going mad. "What *is* this place?" he asked himself aloud.

A large group of cobras gathered around Mandihar when

he arrived and were now engaged in what seemed to be a serious conversation. One of them had been watching Pharaoh and now glided to his side.

"This must seem strange to you," he said in a deep hiss.

Still shaking inside, Pharaoh turned to look at this huge presence with hood extended, elegant but with the same cold, predatory eyes as Mandihar.

"More than strange," Pharaoh barely managed to say.

The elder cobra did not give his name but never diverted his gaze from Pharaoh's eyes. Pharaoh felt an intense knot in his stomach, but he returned the gaze as steadily as he could.

"And I know you are Pharaoh. Mandihar has told us about you over the years."

Pharaoh remained silent.

"To answer the question you just asked, this is the real snake world at the top . . . the world of power and control."

"Power and control?" Pharaoh asked while never looking away from the pens.

The elder snake smiled at Pharaoh's intrigue. "Yes . . . power and control."

The mass of snakes continued in their furor as the two looked on.

"Where are these snakes from?" asked Pharaoh.

"Let's just say this is their only home and leave it at that."

Pharaoh's mind quickly tried piecing together all that he had witnessed in the few days of training with Mandihar. A few things stood out, especially all the snakes working in the outside garden with his former missing classmate. His thoughts were interrupted by the echoing of a snapping whip off the cavern walls. The pit erupted into "to grow limbs." The old snake let out a laugh as he watched the performance below.

The old cobra said unexpectedly, "How can you get limbs?" Pharaoh was caught completely off guard and hesitated.

"We will kill HOXD!" the cobra screamed, and then burst into diabolical laughter. "WE WILL KILL HOXD!" he screamed once more for emphasis.

Something resonated in Pharaoh's brain as this strange, yet familiar-sounding battle cry echoed off the basalt walls of this ancient place. He relaxed a bit and felt a kinship with this old cobra. He sat back and took pleasure in the surroundings.

Mandihar and several other cobra friends were just returning from their monthly inspection tour of the many dens in the underground caverns of Cobra Crucible. They always gave special scrutiny to dens occupied by females: breeders, caretakers of the young and old, cooks, den keepers . . . all attendants to the needs and demands of the males. In ancient times, female snakes were often portrayed as symbols of wisdom, healing, and fertility. Mandihar had to make certain these females would never revert to such foolish notions. Special attention was also given to the pens filled with young garters used for experiments with plants grown in Moon Meadow.

Upon his return, Mandihar gave an almost imperceptible nod to the anonymous cobra, who quietly left Pharaoh's side while Pharaoh intently watched the pens erupt in a frenzy. Mandihar caught Pharaoh's attention and motioned for him to follow the old wizard into the tunnel for the journey back to Moon Meadow. Again, Pharaoh caught a quick glimpse of a silver-and-green streak out of the corner of his eye. This time he was certain; but when he turned, there was nothing.

Gaia peered down the darkening tunnel from beneath a small rock in the tunnel wall of Cobra Crucible where she had been watching and listening. She was scared to death of being discovered by the cobras and cursed herself for having followed Pharaoh here. When Mandihar had summoned Pharaoh to his cavern, she just had to see what was going on. The next morning, she had gone to Mandihar's Cavern to spy. She hung around for quite a while, but it was totally quiet. She went home and returned the next day just as Mandihar and Pharaoh were entering the secret tunnel to Cobra Crucible. Impulsively, she followed them. Now, the darkness of the twisting tunnels terrified Gaia, and she knew if she veered off, she may never find her way out again.

Pharaoh and Mandihar were moving speedily; Pharaoh's tail grew small. She looked around before leaving her hiding spot. Four big cobras were coiled just a few feet away, watching what was going on in the pens below. In sheer panic, she slowly came out from under the rock and hugged the wall until the tunnel darkened somewhat, only then daring to look behind her. No cobra was following her. She slithered into the darkness faster than she ever had in her life and soon had Pharaoh faintly in sight. A wave of uneasiness spread through her body as she slithered along, recalling the change she saw in Pharoah's posture when he was with Mandihar: from cowering to upright and confidant when he spoke with his mentor. When they reached the exit hole, Gaia hung back and watched them exit the tunnel—slithering off, chatting like old friends—toward Mandihar's cavern. When they were out of sight, Gaia followed their exit and headed for home.

The path home seemed longer than usual today. Many working snakes passed by on the way to the river for their lunch break, chatting about everyday commonalities. In the past few days, Gaia's world had expanded but Moon Meadow seemed the same. This made her feel disconnected as she made her way home.

CHAPTER 23

KIMBA SURPRISES GAIA

What Gaia had seen and heard at Cobra Crucible changed her forever, but she tried to seem as normal as possible when she returned home. Pharaoh was with Mandihar. Her family was in turmoil.

Today she was at school and sitting alone outside during lunch break. All the craziness over the last few days took away her appetite. It was soothing for her to bask in the warm sun as she tried to sort out what had happened. A group of Pharaoh's friends slithered by, chatting and laughing.

They are clueless, Gaia thought as she worried about her brother. Scenarios ran through her mind repeatedly as she tried to understand how it came to be that her family could no longer communicate. Why did the light go out in Pharaoh's eyes? Gaia had no answers, only an ominous feeling that something was very wrong.

A voice broke into her troubled thoughts.

"Hi, G-G-Gaia."

"Hi, Kimba."

When she looked up, it took a moment for her eyes to adjust to the bright sunlight. Kimba appeared different. He was nervously slithering around and was not looking at her directly. He spoke more quickly and louder.

"Where's your f-f-f-friend?" he said in an agitated way.

Gaia paused and felt confused. "Lucima?" Gaia had been so preoccupied with Pharaoh that she hadn't even thought about why Lucima wasn't in class. Alarm set in.

"I don't know. Maybe she's sick?"

Kimba looked around to make sure no one was listening. "That's not w-w-what I heard."

"I'm so confused, Kimba. What's going on?"

Now he coiled up closer to Gaia and lowered his voice. "I n-n-n-need to tell you s-s-something."

Kimba then repeated everything he had overheard that morning when Lucima's mom had told Miss Hissy about why Lucima wouldn't be back in school for a long time. Miss Hissy had been very upset.

Gaia really had trouble processing this and was in shock. She finally spoke in a faint, flat voice. "I knew I shouldn't have left her alone."

"W-w-what do y-y-you mean?"

Gaia's posture slumped as she realized she now had to explain some of this to Kimba. But how do you explain an enormous python with legs and arms and a purple third eye who is somehow possibly related to an old, mysterious neighborhood garter without sounding quite crazy? And that was just the beginning. Gaia could not unsee what she had seen nor unhear what she had heard. Yet could she expect others to believe it? She didn't want Kimba to think she was totally crazy. She really, really liked him.

"Well . . ." Gaia said. .

Kimba drew his head closer to Gaia, almost touching her face.

Gaia knew then how much she liked Kimba, for even in her pain, she prayed to Serpens that she did not have day-old toad breath.

"Well," she said again before telling Kimba in part what happened. The rest would come in time. She told him everything that happened in her and Lucima's adventure to Kukulkan. She said that she had gone into the forbidden area to explore it, but Lucima was scared and went home. She didn't mention her ascent of Kukulkan Tower and all that had happened. Even being told only that part of the story, Kimba sat stunned as Gaia finished.

Gaia waited for a reply, but Kimba was speechless. He wanted to speak but was still trying to process all the details. Finally, Gaia spoke. "So Lucima is at Mandihar's cave?"

"Y-y-yes."

Both sat in silence. Gaia felt a sense of relief at sharing her story, especially with Kimba.

Miss Hissy's loud voice broke the moment.

"Back to class everyone."

All the snakes began wiggling their way toward the school.

Kimba hung back, wanting to say something.

"G-G-Gaia . . ."

Gaia's inquisitive brown eyes waited for him to finish.

"I r-r-r-really like you."

Gaia didn't move. A big ray of sunshine pushed aside the darkness in her soul.

"Come on, E6 and C5. Let's go," yelled Miss Hissy as she turned and entered the school.

Gaia still didn't move. She just sat wide-eyed.

Kimba smiled as he leaned in and brushed his soft mouth against hers. He slowly pulled back and gazed into her eyes. Gaia's nose twitched slightly as Kimba tilted his head and gave a shy little smile. She finally found her words.

"I really like you too," Gaia said shyly.

Together, they slithered back to class.

CHAPTER 24

MANDIHAR'S ARMY

Gaia lay on the path in front of her den. When she returned home from school, no one was home, so she decided to enjoy the warmth of the late afternoon sun. Kimba's kiss kept replaying in her mind. Tingles spread through her scales as she tried to decide which was softer, his touch or his eyes. She squirmed at the memory. It was killing her to not be able to tell Lucima.

Oh, Lucima, Gaia thought, *I hope you are OK.*

Gaia's euphoria evolved into worry as she thought about Lucima being in Mandihar's correctional facility. She would try again to talk to her mother.

Loud voices coming down the path cut her worry short. She slithered to the side of the walkway. Two large cobra patrols slithered toward her with a small garter between them.

"Move it," yelled one of the cobras to the garter trying to keep pace.

"You're never going to make it if you don't pick it up," the other cobra said.

Both cobras snickered as they approached Gaia.

"Kimba?" Gaia asked in a horrified voice.

Kimba's fearful yellow eyes penetrated Gaia.

"What's going on?" Gaia yelled in a shrill voice.

Neither cobra broke their stride, pushing Kimba with them.

"Th-th-they are t-t-aking—"

"Shut up," yelled one of the cobras as he swatted the back of Kimba's neck with his tail.

Gaia shuddered at the impact.

"Da-da-da-da. Where did you learn to speak, buddy?" taunted the other cobra, sending both cobras into a fit of laughter.

Kimba hung his head low as he struggled to keep up.

"*Kimba!*" Gaia shrieked at the top of her lungs.

Both cobras stopped short, causing Kimba to stumble. "You keep it up, little girl, and you will be next," one said, then paused as he looked into Gaia's eyes. A leering grin spread across his cruel face.

"Oh, I get it. He's your sweetheart," he said and let out a diabolical laugh.

"Well, he won't be around this full moon to smoochie-smoochie with."

Gaia went silent.

"Yeah, that's what I thought, you little brat!"

Gaia watched in shock as the three headed down the path until they were out of sight.

Mandihar sat before a large group of newly captured young male snakes who were hissing vehemently.

"Please, everyone settle down," he said in a calm manner above the clamor.

The roar of hisses continued.

"I said quiet!" he now yelled in an authoritative voice.

Silence immediately enveloped the large meadow near Cobra Crucible where Mandihar's army trained.

"As you all know, the normal age to join the army is fifteen." The sea of snake heads bobbed up and down in unison. "Due to certain unavoidable circumstances, that age is now twelve."

Chatter exploded from the young snakes. Mandihar's large crew of cobra guards all snapped their powerful tails on the ground, and a hush fell over the crowd.

"You will all stay here for a short period of training, and you will not have any contact with anyone other than those here today."

Kimba looked around at the other snakes sitting next to him, trying to piece together what was happening.

"Once the training is over, the mission will begin." Mandihar slithered to the side, allowing one of his guards to take over. "All right everyone, let's go!"

Next Full Moon

After the brief training period, on the morning of Full-moonday, Mandihar aligned his troops in three strategic rows. The old veterans coiled, still and at attention, while the young captives shifted uneasily, garnering Mandihar's disapproving look. Next to him, before the troops, was Pharaoh, who had been appointed Mandihar's second-in-command for the coming battle.

"Let's get HOXD!" screamed Mandihar as the troops were ready to begin their journey.

The route they would take wound through this large meadow and came out on the far side of Kukulkan, still in the highlands but which soon dropped precipitously into the huge crater where the tower stood. On the edge of this cliff was a large expanse of reed grasses, which allowed intruders to remain unseen and assured an easier entry into the tower.

Mandihar had Pharaoh give the official order to begin, and the troops began disappearing into the tall meadow grasses.

Gaia, too, had gotten up early on Fullmoonday. She had run every scenario she could imagine through her mind repeatedly, but one stood out. She kept hearing the cobra guard's voice saying Kimba wouldn't be around this full moon. Then, when the snakes of Moon Meadow were all whispering about young males suddenly disappearing over the last few days, she felt certain that Mandihar was gathering an army to attack HOXD—when the moon was full. She felt she should warn HOXD. He, after all, had spared her life.

Gaia left Moon Meadow before the sun was fully risen. She was going to take the new, unfamiliar route through the meadow she had discovered and wanted to give herself extra time. She had no desire to cross the Avenue of the Dead again.

Her new route was shaded and cool. Gaia took a few wrong turns but was always able to right herself. And now, in the distance, the late afternoon sun was shining on Kukulkan.

Suddenly, Gaia felt something. A rumble in the earth that coursed through her whole body. It seemed like something large was moving quickly in her direction. She was frightened and sped off as fast as she could toward Kukulkan, the rumbling following her all the way.

She reached the long stairway leading to the rooftop of Kukulkan Tower and sat gasping, trying to catch her breath. And then she saw, not far away, a swath of tall grasses—the very ones she had just passed through—swaying rhythmically and progressively in a line toward the tower. Mandihar's advance troops had arrived. She could see, but not clearly, that it was the young troops in the first line of assault now emerging from the grasses and sliding down the steep drop-off into the sandy crater. She watched in horror as one young snake faltered and fell, and a huge cobra fell on his back. The young snake stopped moving. The cobra flicked him off to the side with his tail and moved on. Gaia felt sick, but things were moving quickly, and she had to find cover. She looked back at the injured snake as she left and saw that he was moving a little. But she couldn't hear his scream.

"Heeelllp mmmmmeeee."

Mandihar's army was now encroaching swiftly. Gaia had to decide right now if she would try to get up the stairs ahead of the army, but knew she couldn't. A small, broken piece of rock lay at the bottom of the stairway. Instinctively, Gaia dove behind it. The sun continued to fade as small garters and cobras began passing by the rock where Gaia hid and began slithering their way up the stairs in a steady stream.

Gaia looked down the line of invading snakes, desperately looking for Kimba. She still hadn't seen him when there were only about twenty small garters and cobras left. Soon the medium-sized and bigger snakes would arrive; she knew that to have any chance of blending in, she had to make her move now. She slithered out from behind the rock and joined the last of the garters. No one seemed to notice. As Gaia kept moving with the army of snakes trying to figure out her next move, her mind was a whirlwind as she tried keeping up with the snakes that slithered in unison, their eyes fixed straight ahead. As she got higher up on the stairs, she looked back and saw a seemingly endless line of variegated colors with large, powerful venomous snakes silently bringing up the rear.

After a few minutes, all the invading troops were on the stairs. The sun dropped lower, further closing the gap to the horizon, and creating a beam of light that illuminated the stairs' entrance. It was almost magical. Something familiar caught Gaia's eye and sparked her curiosity. The small dot quickly morphed into two figures—one large and the other small. A burning feeling filled her stomach as she swallowed hard. Gaia immediately recognized her brother's swagger. *Dear brother, what have you done?*

Mandihar and Pharaoh confidently slithered side by side with an air of authority. The rooftop's silent activity drew Gaia's attention away from her brother. Little heads sought cover in any nook available; Gaia quickly followed by slithering into a crevice close to the inner stairway. Every space filled quickly, forcing the larger cobras to remain on the stairs. They crouched their sizeable bodies out of view as Mandihar and Pharaoh joined them. An unnatural hush fell over the ancient tower as everyone waited for the emergence of HOXD.

Kukulkan was coming to the end of a normal day. HOXD sat overlooking the workers dispersing back to their sleeping quarters after a grueling day of labor. He waited patiently for the last snake to slither out of sight down the long corridor before he rose from his "throne" and stretched. He surveyed the room one last time and checked on the infant snakes in Centralia before making his way to the rooftop stairway. He couldn't wait to bathe in the moon's healing light and restore his sore, heavy limbs. He really needed a recharge.

HOXD was halfway up the rooftop stairway when a voice from below called out his name. He stopped his ascent and looked to see who was calling him, but the spreading darkness obscured his field of vision. He took a step backward for a better view just as the last ray of sunlight reflected off Meteor's bicep, illuminating the embedded rock.

"Oh, yes, Meteor. What is it?"

"I just wanted to give you a quick update on my progress with the atomizer."

"Ah, yes, the atomizer." HOXD's interest was sparked. "How is it coming?"

"Really well. I—" Meteor replied as he took a step closer.

The sun made its final descent below the horizon, and the sudden blackness in the stairway made HOXD cut Meteor short.

"Sorry, but we will have to catch up in the morning."

Without another word, he lumbered up the stairs in eager anticipation of the healing light of the full moon.

CHAPTER 25

WAR ON THE ROOFTOP

Gaia couldn't stop shaking as she waited in the tight, suffocating crevice.

A familiar loud, slow thud stopped Gaia's racing mind; it was a noise still fresh in her memory. She held her breath while watching the towering HOXD emerge into the night, his impressive size illuminated in the full moon's waxing light.

Gaia watched Pharaoh's mouth gape at the sight of HOXD, as he vigorously shook his head, while the giant adjusted himself on the rock slab. Gaia saw the same kindness radiating from his eyes that she had witnessed the other night.

Then, the chant began.

"Oh, energy of the universe
Make me whole
A part of all living things
All that is breathing
All energy
Send us light out of darkness
Order out of chaos
My soul is open to you."

An eerie silence hung over Kukulkan as the moonlight bounced off the giant creature's bare legs. Gaia scanned the rooftop from her cramped space next to the staircase. Along with Mandihar's troops, she eagerly awaited a signal.

It wasn't long before loud snoring broke the quiet air. Out of the corner of her eye Gaia saw Mandihar raise his inflated hood high. A rush of small garters emerged first, swiftly moving toward HOXD. Gaia held back because she wasn't sure what was going on. Frantically, she scanned the roof's entirety, trying to figure out where to fit in. And that was when she saw him. A muscular garter snake with limbs. His checkered yellow body was small but stout with arms and legs that moved like a Leg Walker. He busily began setting something up. She tried twisting her head for a better view, but the corner of a wall blocked Gaia's full line of vision. She felt like she was going crazy as she tried keeping up with the escalating scene.

The frenzied movements of the small garters made Gaia refocus her attention on HOXD. They split up into four groups, quietly arranging themselves next to HOXD's wrists and ankles. Gaia sensed that her window of opportunity was closing. Immediately, she slipped in with the last group as they passed her. She had to sprint to keep up with them as they arranged themselves near HOXD's ankles. Gaia sat catching her breath as the medium-size garters and cobras glided quickly to his biceps and thighs.

Lastly, all but a few of the gigantic cobras strategically positioned themselves near HOXD's chest and abdomen. All sat perfectly still in their assigned spots looking towards Mandihar. A flurry of movement surrounded Gaia as a quick, definitive nod from the wizard set the snakes in orchestrated motion.

Gaia was jostled around in all the movement, finding herself being pushed up higher on HOXD's calf, as the snakes began interlacing with each other all the way up his legs. Gaia watched HOXD's skin disappear under the tightly woven snake blanket. She was amazed at the swiftness of the snakes as they connected to each other and around the rock platform. Once all were securely interconnected, they paused for their final command. Gaia jumped at the deafening snap of Mandihar's tail as she immediately felt the two connecting snakes constrict.

Instantly, HOXD snapped out of his slumber and attempted to sit up. His body thrashed underneath Gaia as he tried freeing himself from being confined. She watched as all the garters near her clung on tightly, their eyes bulging from exertion, as they rolled up and down HOXD's massive legs. Gaia held on with all her might, catching a glimpse of HOXD's panicked eyes, as he lifted his head a few inches off the platform.

HOXD's third eye doubled in size at the sight of the multicolor garter blanket draped over him. A wave of guilt swept over Gaia at seeing the anguish in his face. Everything was occurring so quickly she still wasn't sure how to help him. Her shame intensified as HOXD's struggle continued.

A silhouette came into her peripheral vision. The large, inflated hood made its way towards HOXD's head. Suddenly, Gaia felt like the floor had dropped out from beneath her as HOXD's muscles relaxed. He let out a loud defeated sigh.

"Mandihar . . . I should have known."

A low, sinister, raspy chuckle polluted the beautiful night-time air. "Yes, HOXD, you should have. Your security measures are inferior. But then, you have always thought you were invincible, an immortal." Mandihar paused while giving HOXD a disgusted look. "You live alone and must answer to no one. But tonight you do have to answer—to me," he hissed.

"What is it you want, Mandihar?" HOXD asked between shallow breaths.

Mandihar's diabolical laugh sent shivers down Gaia's spine as his eyes narrowed, making them appear blacker.

"You know very well what I want," he hissed in a menacing way. "The information you have held secret all this time."

Gaia wondered what information Mandihar was talking about. She tried to find Pharaoh to see his reaction, but all she saw was a huge black hood.

A small wave rolled under Gaia again as HOXD continued pulling at the restraints. His voice grew angry, "Never ever will I give you such information."

Mandihar chuckled at his enemy's struggle. "We will see, HOXD, we will see. By the way, how are you feeling without the moonlight? Hmmm . . . feeling a little weak, are you?" A slow smile spread, exposing Mandihar's two gargantuan, stained, yellow fangs.

Mandihar continued taunting HOXD as he slowly slithered around the platform. Gaia sensed Mandihar was soaking up the moment at having HOXD helpless and dependent on him. The way he kept pausing every few feet and smiling arrogantly was too much for her to take. She wanted to do something . . . scream, slither, anything . . .

Instead, she sat still and helplessly watched Mandihar's scheming mind at work, disgusted by the flicking of his tongue.

As Mandihar passed yet again the mat of garters on HOXD's legs, he stopped short. Gaia's heart skipped a beat.

"What is this?" Mandihar asked.

Gaia surveyed the snakes around her to see what was wrong. She saw a mat composed of many rows of compressed garters, each row matching the one above in a repeating pattern, head to tail. What could it be?

Then, it hit her. Gaia felt sick with the realization of her mistake. She was tail to tail! *I am out of order*, she screamed to herself.

Maybe if she believed she were head to tail she would magically transform. She repeated to herself inside, *Head to tail . . . head to tail . . .*

Every passing second was pure torture.

A large, hooded head swooped within inches of her face as hot rat breath stung her eyes. Gaia felt faint as she looked at Mandihar's huge, pointed teeth hanging right over her. One swoop and she would be a goner. The thought triggered her survival instinct, which caused her body to release a horrific, musky odor.

"Who is this little one?" Mandihar said as he gasped from the stench.

Mandihar's head came even closer, his tongue almost touching Gaia. She had a close-up of his last meal, brown remnants stuck in his teeth.

"Come here, Pharaoh. I think we have an imposter . . . or

a rebel."

Mandihar suddenly was gone, bending over at HOXD's side, returning with her brother perched on his back. Pharaoh's jaw dropped at the sight of his sister. He motioned with his eyes trying to communicate. Gaia didn't know how to respond.

"Well . . ." Mandihar said, "Do you know her?"

Pharaoh's voice cracked slightly as he responded. "That is my little sister,"

"Your sister? You mean Gaia? E6?" Mandihar roared.

Gaia's nose began twitching uncontrollably. All she could think of was Miss Hissy's list. Pharaoh fumbled for words; Gaia hoped he would think of something believable to say. "I asked her to join our mission. I knew you needed as many of us as possible."

Mandihar's temper exploded. He thrust his head down to the floor and gave it a swift flick, and Gaia watched Pharoah fly into the hard rock wall. He winced with the impact, but quickly sat up. Mandihar loomed largely over him.

"You decided this on your own?" Mandihar's anger rose with the accusation.

Gaia's stomach was in knots as she watched her brother receive Mandihar's wrath. "I . . . I . . . didn't think it was a big deal."

"It is a huge deal! You have breached our security!" Mandihar slithered in a large circle as he tried sorting out his mind. "I was warned about Gaia being a menace. All her questions . . ."

"Mandihar, I was just trying to help you. I swear," Pharaoh said.

"Sorry, are you? We'll see about that."

Mandihar turned and thrust his big face right in front of Gaia's. She gagged from his breath as he shrieked for her to get down. Instantly, the snakes surrounding her gave her room to leave, their frightened eyes averted. She wriggled free, dropped to the floor, and in a flash, slithered over to Pharaoh. The evilness shooting from Mandihar's eyes terrified her.

"So, you know what you must do," Mandihar said to Pharaoh in a subdued, calm voice. Mandihar loomed over Pharaoh and Gaia with his hood fully extended. An ominous shadow hovered over the trembling brother and sister.

Pharaoh gave Mandihar a puzzled look.

"Kill her," Mandihar said in a voice without emotion.

Gaia opened her mouth wide to scream, but nothing came out.

"What?" exclaimed Pharaoh.

"I said, kill her!"

Gaia tried to yell again and this time an explosive wail vibrated off the boulders.

Mandihar paused briefly before bursting into a fit of laughter.

"Kill who?"

Mandihar's maniacal laughter thundered off the walls of Kukulkan, echoing in the cool night air. "Who? Oh you are a funny boy aren't you." Mandihar's laughter abruptly stopped; his face grew fiendish. "Kill Gaia."

The air grew muskier. Suddenly everything seemed to be in slow motion as Gaia's fear came to a crescendo.

"Kill your sister, or both of you will die!" Mandihar now

shouted.

Pharaoh looked paralyzed. Gaia was shocked as her brother was rendered speechless.

"You must show your loyalty to regain my trust, Pharaoh. I want you to hold her down, and then I will come and sink my fangs into her."

Serpens! Where are you? Please help me! Gaia shrieked to herself. *Save me please!*

Pharaoh snapped out of his paralysis, his voice full of desperation. "But Mandihar . . . I am loyal. Please don't hurt my sister! Please!" He pleaded for his sister's life, but Gaia knew it was useless.

"Subdue her now!" Mandihar's mouth curled into a ghoulish smile, his long, pink tongue flicking in and out.

Mandihar's black eyes penetrated Gaia's while her sense of time became warped as she prepared to die. Everything was happening hastily, yet she felt like she was floating in slow motion. Reality no longer had any meaning. Inside, she was shrieking for her family. She wanted to tell them all how much she loved them and that she was sorry for leaving. She tried to meet her brother's eyes, but Pharaoh looked like he was frantically scanning the area for an out.

CHAPTER 26

MANDIHAR MEETS THE ATOMIZER

At the base of the tower, Asmodeus slithered around in the sparse weeds, trying to find the best spot to hear what was going on up on the roof. He had been driven out of his den in the field of reeds by Mandihar's army of huge cobras who rampaged through the field, rolling over the edge of the cliff where Asmodeus hid in a small crevice on its underside. He was totally bewildered as he watched the army ascend on Kukulkan Tower. Terrified, he waited but then followed. Short bursts of loud, angry yelling floated down the nearby stairway, so he headed there. Quickly, he sought refuge behind a large boulder. Wailing cries came from above. Asmodeus felt helpless. Out of nowhere, his purple eye twitched.

Oh no, not again, he said to himself. The familiar aura of flashing lights began. "Please, not now." He bartered with whoever would listen, this time out loud.

His pleading went unanswered.

At the edge of HOXD's vision, he could still see Mandihar yelling at Pharaoh and Gaia.

"You'd better make up your mind or I will make it up for you, Pharaoh," Mandihar hissed. HOXD was sure Gaia was the same snake that had intruded on his platform during the last full moon. There was no mistaking those soft mocha eyes. And now she had thrown a wrench into the wizard's evil plan. This brought HOXD hope. Time was of the essence as he felt the effect of the smothering garter blanket across his legs. He could feel his energy draining with every passing minute as he looked up at the sky for help, hoping he retained enough energy to connect with the lunar beam. HOXD strained as his purple eye locked its sight on the moon. The power surge began as his eyes twitched. Mandihar's loud shouting grew distant as HOXD moved into another dimension.

Pressure began building, and Asmodeus' third eye spasmed. An unbearable force came from the direction of the rooftop. He clung to the ground as he tried to resist the force pulling at the back of his head. It seemed the universe was intent on showing him something he didn't understand, despite his resistance. He fought against it, swinging his head every which way; he did not want to give in. Suddenly, a light-blue beam zigzagged from his third eye, following the same direction as the intense pressure. Asmodeus's strength was depleting rapidly as he begrudgingly gave in to the unknown power. His head snapped back with his eyes staring straight up the staircase. Vibrations shook his head with each jolt of energy.

HOXD gathered what little energy he had left. Without warning, Gaia's body lifted off the rock floor a few inches and hovered momentarily. Mandihar shook his head in seeming disbelief. As quickly as she was in the air, she returned to the ground. HOXD shuddered from exhaustion. His purple eye-lid fluttered briefly, uncontrollably, before subsiding to its lazy gaze, focusing intently on lifting Gaia to safety. A slight vibration resonated throughout the rooftop as HOXD drew all the power the universe allowed. Suddenly, Gaia rose again, high above Mandihar. She levitated briefly before crashing to the ground. HOXD's head snapped back as he spent his last reserves. A light tingling sensation crept over his legs as he felt them beginning to wither.

As he lay shaking, Asmodeus followed the blue, quivering beam to the rooftop, but a projecting rock in the wall blocked his view. The surge of energy intensified. A crackling blue haze surrounded him, and just like the other night, he was paralyzed, unable to dissipate the horrifying pressure. A deafening explosion went off in his head as everything went black. Slowly, the blue haze faded, leaving Asmodeus alone in the dark.

HOXD watched as Mandihar appeared insane with rage at the events unfolding, shooting him a piercing look as he shouted, "You see that, Pharaoh? Remember what I told you about the secret information HOXD has?"

Before Pharaoh could respond, Mandihar screamed to HOXD, "Tell me how you did that?" HOXD remained silent, too drained to reply. Mandihar continued to unravel. "Tell me now!"

Finally, HOXD gathered the strength to reply. "Never will I tell you . . . Even if I die, you will always be crawling around on that belly of yours."

Mandihar's frustration was apparent as he slithered in a large circle while ranting, "I must have your knowledge! No more secrets!"

Spit flew from Mandihar's mouth as he turned his attention back to Pharaoh. "Are you ready to obey now?"

Pharaoh sat motionless.

"Well? Are you?" Mandihar thundered as he slithered closer.

"I will not do what you are asking," Pharaoh hissed. "I will not kill my sister."

Silence like a tomb fell over the rooftop. HOXD watched in desperation, but his depleted energy left him incapable of helping. Mandihar slithered closer to Gaia and Pharaoh as they inched backwards.

As Mandihar began to coil before them in strike position, Gaia and Pharaoh entwined their tales while shaking uncontrollably.

"You see HOXD," Mandihar said as he kept his eyes locked on the terrified brother and sister, "You could have prevented this . . ."

Loud voices jolted Asmodeus into an upright position. He rubbed his tail over his forehead, trying to quell the throbbing behind his third eye. Gut-wrenching screams rang down the stairs to where he sat. Clanking noises ricocheting down the stairs exacerbated the pulsating pain in his head, forcing Asmodeus to slither-hop toward his refuge in the reeds.

A soft whimpering stopped him in his tracks. As Asmodeus listened, the whimpering became a continuous moaning coming from behind him to the right. He squinted through the darkness and began moving cautiously toward the sound when angry voices from the rooftop compelled him to pick up his pace.

Before him lay a small garter wrapped loosely in an awkward coil, biting his side. The garter looked up, his huge yellow eyes wide at the sight of a purple eye coming straight at him. He tried to scream.

"N-n-n-n-," he stuttered.

"Ssh! It's OK!" Asmodeus carefully moved closer. "I'm here to help you."

The injured garter tried seeking refuge by hiding his head under his coil, but the pain was unbearable. He fell limply to his side, writhing in pain.

As the voices from the roof grew louder, Asmodeus bent down close to the garter's contorted body. His scales were full of abrasions along his middle back. Small dark-brown spots speckled his bruised right side.

"I think you broke some ribs." Asmodeus looked up as he heard the violence escalating. "We gotta get outta here."

The garter looked up; his yellow eyes were now dull as they looked at Asmodeus. He seemed scared and confused but too weak to fight.

Asmodeus tested the little snake's trust as he took another slither-hop closer. He lay still, so Asmodeus moved over to him and bent over. "What's your name?"

The small snake looked like it took all his strength to respond. "K-k-k-imba," he stuttered.

"This might hurt for a minute," Asmodeus warned as he curled his tail around Kimba and hoisted him onto his back.

Kimba grimaced and yelped.

"Sorry, little guy."

Carefully, Asmodeus worked his way to the cliff. Kimba shuddered with every hop. A deafening, swooshing noise blew over from the rooftop, followed by horrified screams. Asmodeus gave Kimba a boost and told him to hold on as he quickly climbed the cliff's wall. An agonizing scream erupted from Kimba, but it could barely be heard over the grim sounds of war breaking out on the tower's roof.

Asmodeus quickly hauled Kimba over to the grass bed and gently laid him down. Kimba rolled over in a peculiar position, his eyes never losing contact with Asmodeus's purple eye.

"Th-th-thank—" Kimba's head fell forward as he passed out.

It seemed to Gaia like eternity had passed since she and Pharaoh sat coiled before Mandihar.

She had feared her spirit was on its way to the next life when she had spontaneously lifted into the air. Her time on earth seemed to have run its course. But then the hard impact of the rooftop reminded her she was still alive. For how long, though, she did not know. Hatred oozed from Mandihar's icy stare as he hovered high above her and her brother. He seemed to salivate from his exuding power. Gaia kept backing up to the outside stairway, only to find four large cobras blocking the steps below. The walls of her world came crashing in as she realized nothing could save her.

She leaned her nose toward Pharaoh's and whispered, "I love you."

Pharaoh's voice cracked as he replied, "Me too."

Gaia tensed, waiting for the inevitable. A sudden movement by the inner stairwell caught her eye. Before she had time to gather her thoughts, a blurred figure holding a strange contraption came storming towards her. As it got closer, Gaia recognized the yellow-checkered snake with arms and legs from earlier. His eyes looked directly through her as he sprinted by.

Mandihar's self-satisfied smirk had transformed into abject fear. Before Gaia could react, the checkered snake raised the strange weapon high. A loud hiss erupted from Mandihar as he lunged towards the oncoming snake. Suddenly, an intense swooshing sound pierced the night air. Gaia heard HOXD scream "Meteor!" as the armed snake swiped his weapon down on Mandihar's neck. A warm sensation spread over Gaia as she was sprayed with blood. She squinted through the mist hanging in the air as Mandihar's body fell lifelessly to the ground, staining the floor a deep maroon. A salty taste filled her mouth as she looked down at her body covered in Mandihar's remains. She threw up on the spot. Time stood still as she stared at the carnage. Nothing moved. Then mayhem erupted.

Gaia remained next to Pharaoh as the war escalated, too afraid to move. Amongst splattered snake parts, Meteor stood at the top of the cavern staircase holding a strange weapon with a long, wide-bore, metal barrel with a huge valve on its base. Attached to the weapon was a tightly woven harness that seemed to stabilize it. Numerous other snakes with arms and legs stood next to him holding similar devices. By the inner staircase, snakes were busy handling a tubelike device made of thousands of long, hollow reeds which connected to an overhead, high-pressure water spigot in the bowels of Kukulkan. An array of snakes with partial limbs assisted. Gaia thought she was hallucinating. Quickly, Pharaoh nudged Gaia to follow him to a tiny crevice close by, and they slithered speedily to safety. They stared at each other wide-eyed but didn't utter a word.

In horror, Gaia watched as a few large cobras slithered speedily toward Meteor. With hoods fully extended, fangs dripping with deadly venom, they coiled and stretched their upper bodies high into the air in strike position. With one quick swoop of his hands, Meteor swung the barrel of the weapon in front of him and flipped the valve. Another series of swooshing sounds penetrated the air as the other snakes swiftly handled the tube from the cavern. Small reddish pieces of razor-sharp sand, mixed with the high-pressure water in a deadly slurry, sliced through the approaching cobras. An explosion of red droplets showered the rooftop. Sporadic swooshing noises continued as the other snakes decimated Mandihar's crew.

Gaia gawked as Mandihar's army fell apart and desperately struggled to exit Kukulkan. Small garters began disassembling the mat on HOXD's legs, dropping to the floor while dodging pelting snake parts as they fled for the stairway. One by one, the cobras around HOXD's chest followed suit.

Pharaoh nudged Gaia. "Come on, let's get out of here."

Gaia couldn't take her eyes off of the chaos but nodded

her head in agreement.

She immediately followed Pharaoh as he wiggled out from the crevice but came to a halt as reddish sand penetrated the rooftop in front of her. The swooshing continued, blocking her path. She tried calling after her brother but knew it was futile. Panic set in, forcing her to turn back and once again dive into the safety of the crevice.

Gaia's stomach sank as she saw two tiny garters suffocate as a cobra slithered its muscular body over them. Pharaoh's tail was all Gaia could still see as she watched it wiggle behind four cobras. Then, it disappeared as Pharaoh flung himself over the top stair. Gaia prayed for his safety.

The last of the snakes vanished down the stairs. The screams lessened as the swooshing sounds slowed pace. Gaia stared in disbelief at the unrecognizable rooftop. She couldn't believe how quickly it had transformed. A slow dripping sound came from above as a small pool of blood formed by her head, which was peeking out of the crevice.

Meteor and his troops continuously swiveled back and forth, scanning the rooftop, their barrels held perfectly in front of them. Gaia's tired eyes followed every movement of the weapon that had saved them. Never had she seen such a terrifying apparatus, not even from the Leg Walkers. She quivered every time it pointed in her direction, petrified it would discharge and turn her into snake dust, never to be found. The shiny object had her transfixed.

Meteor made one last sweep of the rooftop before jumping down from the boulder he was standing on.

"Hey watch it, Alset," he yelled.

"Sorry about that," Alset replied as he stepped out of the way. The two of them wrapped their arms around each other as they stood in silence. Gaia wondered if the wreckage affected them like it did her.

A loud, slow gasp from HOXD startled Gaia. His chest rose and fell erratically while low moans came from his limp body. Meteor and Alset rushed by Gaia's secret hiding spot to tend to HOXD. Gaia sensed they were just as lost as she was.

A low, gravelly whisper, barely audible, emerged.

"I need moonlight . . ."

Words eluded Meteor. He struggled with seeing his mentor so weak and vulnerable, straining to stay awake. Meteor nodded, making intense eye contact that he hoped communicated a deep love and respect that needed no words. HOXD's cloudy eyes glistened for a moment.

"One more thing, Meteor . . ."

Meteor took a slow step forward and lowered his head closer to HOXD's so as not to miss a word. HOXD's eyes rolled side to side.

"One more . . ."

Meteor froze as HOXD's head fell limply to the side.

Alset leaned down and rubbed HOXD's head to see if he could wake him. He looked at Meteor who was still standing like a statue.

"I wonder what he was going to say?"

Meteor shuffled his feet slightly. "Me too . . . me too."

Meteor and Alset tried to figure out if the few remaining hours of moonlight would be enough to restore HOXD's energy. They kept looking up at the sky, searching for an answer. They would point to the moon and then to HOXD and back to the moon.

Finally, Meteor shrugged his shoulders and said, "I guess time will tell."

The two stood guard, patiently waiting to see what the new day would bring.

CHAPTER 27

PHARAOH TAKES CHARGE

On the tower's ground level, chaos ensued as snakes fled in every direction. Pharaoh, his body covered in blood, watched with vacant eyes as mangled snakes slithered by, screaming as they dragged their broken bodies to the reeds above. His mind just couldn't process all that had happened so abruptly. Never in his life had Pharaoh been a leader of anything, and now he watched, paralyzed.

Pharaoh was so immersed in his own desperation that he didn't notice a small group of garters gathering before him. Despite their injuries, one by one they coiled quietly in front of Pharaoh and patiently awaited his instructions. By the time he noticed them, he was met with hundreds of fearful eyes, making him gasp. Seeing their desperation made his heart sink and forced him into action.

Pharaoh quickly slithered up a nearby tall rock and, before speaking, sat for a moment, perched above all the others. He felt his fear slightly subsiding as a sense of power crept into his soul. From out of nowhere, he had a glimmer of understanding of why Mandihar always smirked while sitting on his ledge. Being higher than others was almost intoxicating. It was a fleeting thought, but it bothered Pharaoh that he enjoyed it so much. He cleared his mind and shouted to those below.

"Let's leave the same way we came," he said, pointing with his tail toward the tall reeds. "We will meet up later when it is safe."

All the tiny green heads nodded.

"Let's go!" Pharaoh yelled.

The snakes darted so quickly toward the reeds that a large plume of dust rose in the air, causing Pharaoh to have a coughing fit as he slithered down to the ground.

Pharaoh was still hacking as four huge cobras hung behind. Between gasps for breath, he watched them take in what was happening with lifeless, black eyes. Fleeting images of Mandihar crossed his mind. The iciness of their stares erased Pharaoh's fleeting sense of power. His voice cracked as he tried to feign confidence.

"Come on you guys. Let's get outa here."

The cobras continued speaking to each other, dismissing Pharaoh completely. They looked through him as if he were a ghost. Pharaoh watched in the distance as the last of the garters ducked into the grass; the screams and hissing grew fainter. The cobras began circling frantically in front of the base of the stairs as they plotted their next move. Pharaoh couldn't believe what he heard. They wanted to go back up the stairs to continue Mandihar's mission of attaining HOXD's secret information. Pharaoh took one final glance up the stairs, and it was unnervingly quiet.

Gaia . . . are you still up there? Pharaoh cried out to himself.

He sat staring, hoping his sister would spontaneously emerge, but only blood-stained rock remained. The cobras busily strategized, oblivious to Pharaoh. He knew it would be instant death to attempt going back up there. His heart wanted him to try to find Gaia, but his gut was shrieking to get out of there. The inner turmoil was making him crazy.

Oh, Gaia.

A sudden loud scuffling on the roof made Pharaoh's decision easier. He dug into the ground and left as fast as he could, increasing his speed to catch up to the other garters. He was breathless by the time he reached them, and they all stopped and lay in the grass for a short time, their bellies rapidly rising and falling, and then together they continued the long trek home. Pharaoh looked back to see whether the cobras had changed their minds, but all he could see was the gentle swaying of the grass.

Spit was flying in every direction as the cobras spoke heatedly among themselves. Their muscular bodies surged with adrenaline, yet no one made the first move up the stairs. Deep down, they all knew they would be outnumbered and killed if they attempted to continue the fight. They would have to regroup at Cobra Crucible to form a new plan and complete the mission. Their hate-filled eyes narrowed as they spoke. It was unanimous. They would have to leave for now and come back. Then they would do whatever it took to take HOXD down. The four grew increasingly agitated at the thought of killing HOXD. Before leaving, they all dripped a globule of their poisonous venom onto the stairs as a sign of what was to come. One of them started to go toward the grass, but another one shouted for him to stop.

"Let's go this way. It's shorter," he said as he pointed his head over the bare, sandy area.

The cobra turned around and headed in the direction of the other three. Their wide bodies glided over the dried fissures with ease, barely even noticing them. In no time, they had reached the muddy section right before the fence. As Kukulkan began receding into the distance, a sense of relief swept over the cobras and they began talking. But after a few seconds, they all sensed that something wasn't right and conversation ceased. Their slithers slowed down to the point where they were barely moving. Panic could be seen in each other's eyes as they sensed some force larger and more powerful than themselves. Deafening, agonizing screams punctured the quiet night. The cobras' large heads began whipping around in frenzied circles as they fought an invisible force sucking them into the depths. A deep mass of loose sand mixed with water was quickly submerging the massive, muscular cobras with only their heads remaining above the bog. Their once cold, narrow eyes were now dilated with vulnerability and fear. Then, the Avenue of the Dead performed its magic act and made them disappear, without a trace, into the ooze forever. It bubbled a few times before turning still, waiting as it had for millennia for its next victims.

CHAPTER 28

HOXD'S STRUGGLE

Bright, vivid bursts of orange light danced in HOXD's sleeping mind. His head jerked back and forth as random images flashed briefly in his brain before shattering into tiny pieces, floating out of view. The imagery started firing faster, oranges and reds transforming into strange configurations that reached out to him. HOXD winced as if he had been struck. Distant low, muffled voices called to him deep beyond the lights. He couldn't put a name to them, but they sounded familiar. HOXD moved closer to the voices, straining to decipher what was being said.

"HOXD . . ."

In his mind, a blast of orange immediately twisted into a green snake standing before him. Fear coursed through his body as he heard his name being called again.

"HOXD . . .wake up . . ."

The color show in HOXD's mind slowly faded off into the distance as two blurred, shadowy silhouettes came into view. HOXD rubbed his purple eye.

"Wake up!"

Gradually the fuzzy forms hanging over HOXD became clearer. The moonlight disappeared as the two snake heads drew closer, concern etched in their eyes. HOXD's mind took a few seconds to catch up to his sight. Comfort replaced apprehension as he recognized his friends.

"Where am I?"

Alset and Meteor grabbed each other excitedly. Meteor spoke first.

"You are on the roof."

"The roof?"

Alset flashed Meteor a concerned look.

"Yes . . . it's a full moon tonight," Meteor said as he stepped back to let the dazzling light through.

HOXD smiled slightly as the power of the white orb soothed him, bringing him back to the nights long ago he had spent with the shaman. Her image flashed before him sitting at the edge of the platform. He sat up, floundering as he reached out for her. Quickly, Meteor and Alset each grabbed his side.

"Careful . . . you are still weak," said Meteor. While his friend fumbled trying to adjust him, HOXD watched the shaman slowly levitate off the rock. He tried to grab her, but his friend's grip was too tight.

"What is he doing?" asked Meteor.

"I don't know . . . It's like he sees something . . . HOXD, what is it?"

HOXD heard the question but was captivated by the realness of the shaman. Slowly, her figure floated towards the heavens. A slight smile spread across her face before disappearing into the darkness.

Meteor's voice loudened. "Are you OK, HOXD?

HOXD was slow to respond, his mind still slightly fuzzy.

A throbbing ache that pulsated through his legs distracted him. Looking down, he was struck by how his skin had become dull and grey.

A pool of blood by his feet caught his attention. For the first time since waking, he noticed the dried, splattered blood covering the rock before him. He felt bewildered.

"Is it morning?"

"No . . . not for a few more hours."

The crisp air sent a chill down HOXD's back as he tried to make sense of the scene in front of him.

"What happened here?"

"Well . . ." Meteor started hesitantly, "Mandihar brought his crew here and . . ."

A flashback of the battle suddenly came into HOXD's mind as he cut Meteor off.

"Oh yes, Mandihar . . . and that thing." HOXD pointed to the weapon hanging from Meteor's side.

"Yup . . . the atomizer."

It was like a switch flipped on in HOXD's mind. Suddenly, the scenes from the war poured into his mind with over-whelming speed. Then, one image stood out from all the rest, the colors bold and bright: Mandihar's last moment before being sliced in half.

HOXD flinched at the memory. "Mandihar is . . ."

"Dead," Meteor and Alset said in unison.

HOXD was overwhelmed with a confusing mixture of

emotions . . . relief, happiness, and yet sorrow. He shook his head in disbelief.

"We existed for so many years out here—and this is how it ends?" Alset and Meteor stood in silence while HOXD took in the whole rooftop. "So much blood . . . too much . . ." HOXD said, his voice barely audible.

A wave of light-headedness overtook him, and he clutched the sides of the platform.

"You OK?" asked Meteor.

HOXD took a deep breath. "I think so . . . I am still extremely weak."

HOXD turned his tired eyes up to the sky, gauging the moon's location.

"Looks like I have about another hour of moonlight."

"Why don't you lie back down and get some rest? Alset and I will stand guard."

All HOXD wanted to do was sleep, but now a new worry crept into his mind.

"But what if Mandihar's crew comes back?"

Alset looked over the ledge and, trying to sound reassuring, said, "Looks quiet down there. I don't think they will be back."

Meteor nodded. "Ya, but we still need to be prepared for when they do come."

The night was approaching a new day as the three began devising a plan.

CHAPTER 29

GAIA'S CHOICE

Gaia peeked out at the big black boots pacing back and forth just inches from her face. The crevice's cramped space no longer felt like a haven but more like a death trap. Each passing thud of the boots swept in a puff of dust, choking Gaia, but she swallowed hard to suppress the rising tickle in her throat. When she and Pharaoh had rushed into this crevice it had seemed so close to the staircase. Now, however, with three large snakes in the way, it seemed like the other side of Moon Meadow.

Gaia jumped as HOXD called out in a weary voice, "Meteor, you're making me nervous . . . Alset, please make him stop."

Alset motioned to Meteor, but was waved off, and Meteor said, "It's how I think."

Gaia's eyes darted back and forth from Meteor's boots to the stairs, desperately looking for a chance to escape. A long stretch of solid rock spread out for a distance before the crevice opened again right at the top of the stairs. She tried raising her head to see if that crack continued down the stairs, but she couldn't see it clearly. Gaia analyzed the crack while the pacing boots continued. She was out of other options; the crevice was her only hope. Now she just had to wait for the right moment.

The expansive, wide-open space that she had to slither over terrified Gaia. Her addled mind would need a long time to sort out what she had witnessed tonight. The only thing she knew for sure was that HOXD saw her as part of Mandihar's invading army, and she had seen what happened to them. Life was much more complicated now than it was this morning when she set out to help HOXD. And right now, this place terrified her in a whole new way; she had to get out.

A sense of defeat began creeping into her mind, where a conversation was brewing:

Gaia, why did you let this happen? It's because you always have to be so curious, don't you? Well, look at where that has gotten you!

Gaia had no response to her own criticism.

Miss Hissy's immaculate face flooded in. *Gaia, what did I tell you were the two most important traits to possess? Hmmm? Obedience and compliance! If you would have listened to me, you could have had a life with a secure set of limited possibilities, but you threw that dream away!*

Gaia became infuriated with Miss Hissy. *No! No, you are wrong! I don't want to just follow. I want more! It's good to be curious!*

No, it is not! Miss Hissy slowly shook her head. *Have you learned nothing from Mandihar's* Guidance Manual for Young Snake Minds? *Don't question, Gaia, just do as you are told!*

But now I know that the things everyone said were a myth are actually real! I have seen things no one else knows exists.

Oh, Gaia, honey. If you just blindly follow, you don't have to worry your pretty head about what is out there. It is for your own good.

The anger inside Gaia came to a breaking point as she began screaming at Miss Hissy in her mind.

How can you live in a fake world where almost no one speaks the truth?

Miss Hissy's face began fading. *If only you would have followed the rules, Gaia.*

Gaia shouted at the fading phantom of ignorant propriety. *It is good to have a free mind!* Her small body shuddered at the intensity of emotions pulsating through her.

This is not my fault . . . it is not my fault, Gaia told herself as Lucima appeared in her mind.

Gaia, stay strong.

Lucima, I miss you so much! I'd give anything to have you here right now. I am so scared.

You can't leave me, Gaia. I need you. You are my best friend. I need your strength. What would I do without you?

With a poof, Lucima was gone.

A flash of yellow appeared as a muted stutter whispered, *P-p-p-please come home, Gaia. I m-m-m-m-miss you.*

Gaia's heart ached at hearing Kimba's sweet voice. *Oh, Kimba, I miss you too.*

A soft-spoken voice emerged. *Gaia, honey, it is time to come home.*

Mom! Oh, Mom, I want to come home. I am so sorry.

A group of voices from her dad and grandparents joined

her mother.

It's time to come home, Gaia.

I don't know how, Gaia screamed to herself as she shuddered. *I don't know how!*

Come on, Gaia, don't give up. You got this! Think!

Pharaoh stood smiling at her. *Just think, you always find a way out. Don't give up, Gaia.* His voice began trailing off. Slowly he evaporated into a black void. *Don't . . . give . . . up.*

Gaia had become so absorbed in herself that she lost sight of her surroundings. A loud crunching noise snapped her back into the present. The black boots squashed a small pile of pebbles almost directly beneath Gaia's head. A haze spread through the air as a plume of pebble dust engulfed the small, enclosed space.

Gaia tried suppressing an undeniable urge, but couldn't . . . "Hachuuuu!"

All the talking above instantly ceased. Gaia's eyes widened as she held her breath.

"What was that?" Meteor asked. An immense finger pointed right at Gaia.

"Down there. It came from there," said HOXD.

Gaia couldn't believe that after all she had been through, her demise would result from a sneeze.

Two large eyes squinted through the crack.

"Well, well. Would you look at this," Meteor said with a smirk.

Quick, shuffling feet rushed towards Gaia. Now, four black eyes peered in. Fear took hold of Gaia, and her body once again emitted her defensive scent. Both set of eyes immediately winced and pulled out of view.

"What is that smell?" Alset exclaimed.

A stumbling commotion ensued as loud coughing erupted. Gaia immediately saw her chance to flee and wiggled out of her hiding spot, slithering with all her might toward the stairs.

From behind her, she heard HOXD shout, "Get that snake!"

Faster, Gaia, she yelled at herself, all the while keeping her focus on the staircase. Her back, stiff and achy from her confinement in the crevice, swerved back and forth in a flurry. Small vibrations jolted her as the sound of racing footsteps closed in on her. The stairway grew larger with every slither.

Come on, Gaia, go! she screamed at herself.

The shaking beneath her intensified as the stomping became louder. Gaia could feel the boots right next to the tip of her tail.

Meteor rushed past Gaia and stopped right in front of her, causing her to crash into his thick boot. A deafening scream burst into the night, echoing off the battle-scarred rock walls of the rooftop.

"Noooooo!"

Meteor lifted his boot high in the air, hovering over Gaia's trembling body. She shrieked again at the thought of being stomped into oblivion.

"No! Please . . . Nooooo!"

HOXD's voice echoed off the walls. "Stop! Meteor, stop! Don't hurt her!"

Gaia watched, horrified, as Meteor's boot twitched in the air.

"*Don't touch her!*"

Heavy footsteps lumbered slowly towards Gaia. Her body vibrated with every step the three-eyed snake took. Another layer of darkness fell over her as HOXD's immense stature blocked the remaining moonlight. He leaned down, clutching Meteor, and stared into Gaia's eyes. His purple eye appeared dried out as he scrutinized Gaia. Finally, he spoke.

"Don't hurt her," he said one more time, sounding winded. "I can't believe it. Her again."

Meteor slowly brought his foot down to his side with a bewildered look on his face.

"Who is she?"

A slow smile spread across HOXD's exhausted face, reminding Gaia of a crater in the earth.

"Her name is Gaia."

"But *who* is she?"

HOXD looked directly into Meteor's eyes as he spoke. "Well, I am not sure."

Gaia remained rigid, too terrified to move. She watched helplessly as HOXD and Meteor determined her fate. HOXD paused. Gaia wished she knew what he was thinking.

"She is one of us."

"One of us?" Meteor asked, scrunching his face. "But how?"

Suddenly, HOXD's knees buckled. Gaia watched as he swayed back and forth, praying he didn't come crashing down. Meteor and Alset quickly steadied him.

"Come on, HOXD. Let's get you back to your bed," Meteor said, and then quickly added, "Alset, bring Gaia."

As the two turned and slowly stumbled back to the platform, Alset turned his attention to Gaia.

"Come on, Gaia. Move it."

Gaia didn't budge. She could hear everything, but her body wasn't listening to her brain. She tried speaking, but her mouth didn't move. Alset nudged her with his boot, but she just lay there, stiff. With a heavy sigh, he leaned over and picked her up, carrying Gaia over to HOXD and Meteor.

"Man, HOXD, this little friend of yours stinks!"

HOXD laughed weakly as he arranged himself on the rock slab. "She is just scared, Alset. She is just scared."

Alset winced from the strong odor as he asked, "Where do you want her?"

"Just put her down where you are."

Alset bent over and gently set Gaia down by his feet. The coldness from the rock snapped Gaia's body back. Suddenly, she felt she could move, but she didn't dare budge.

"Is she going to be OK?" asked Alset. "She doesn't look so good."

Gaia felt everyone staring at her but kept looking straight up at the moon.

"She is a tough little one. She just needs rest. And so do I," HOXD said.

The will to survive gripped Gaia as she lay listening to the three snakes discussing her destiny. She kept hearing her parents' voices calling her; she had to get home. Very slowly, she turned her head and saw Meteor and Alset watching HOXD as they spoke. Meteor held up his funny-looking weapon to show HOXD. Quietly, she began inching toward the stairs.

Meteor's voice floated toward Gaia.

"But HOXD, you have missed a lot of moonlight."

"And, no offense, but you don't look too good now, either," added Alset.

A sense of hope filled Gaia as the stairs became a reality. She continued inching her way to the exit. A low chortle came from HOXD. "Don't worry, I will be OK."

"But HOXD, I have never seen you this wiped out," Meteor said.

"I know, I can't explain it." HOXD looked up to the sky as he spoke. "It's as if something else was connected to me . . . it was the strangest feeling."

Just as Gaia was nearing the top stair, she heard HOXD's voice grow a bit louder with an unfamiliar sternness.

"Now listen closely. Nothing is to happen to Gaia. Do you understand? I mean *nothing!*"

"Yes sir, we understand." Meteor replied.

"I need you two to stand guard until I wake."

The voices were becoming muffled, but Gaia could still make out Meteor's voice as he replied, "I just have one question, HOXD. Why are we keeping her?"

Gaia's eyes widened as she waited for HOXD to answer.

"Because I must find out what brought her here."

Suddenly, shouting broke out. "She's gone!" Alset screamed.

Gaia was only inches away from freedom; she forced herself to push her stiff body a few more slithers.

"Where did she go?" shouted Meteor.

"Over there, by the stairs!" yelled Alset.

This time Gaia did not look back. She took one last deep breath before flinging herself over the stair's edge, burrowing into the small crevice.

HOXD's distant voice floated down the stairs. "Let her go, Alset! Let her go!"

Gaia snuck a peek back as she followed the crack down the stairs, watching as Alset stopped in his tracks at the top, causing Meteor to crash into him. HOXD's voice faded as he kept repeating, "Let her go . . . let her go."

Gaia burrowed deeper in the crack and worked her way down. Soon, only the sound of chirping crickets filled the night.

CHAPTER 30

GOING HOME

All the garters were gathered in the cavern of Cobra Crucible when Pharaoh arrived. Eagerness exuded from the room full of small black eyes glued to his every move. Then, one by one, their tails started tapping on the hard dirt floor. A roaring clap bounced off the deep cavern walls as the snakes began whistling and chanting.

"Pharaoh . . . Pharaoh . . ." over and over.

Pharaoh tried keeping his mouth from dropping open as he sat in disbelief.

The voices grew louder. "Pharaoh . . . Pharaoh . . ."

He sensed the group wanted him to speak, as if they had already chosen their new leader. Slowly, Pharaoh sat a bit straighter, puffing out his small chest as he enjoyed the newfound confidence building inside. It was a feeling he had only briefly experienced before—that he could do anything.

The shrill screams of battle had receded as Asmodeus tended to Kimba's injuries. Finally, the little snake appeared comfortable, coiled loosely around a mound of cool rocks he had dug from deep in the field of reeds. Helping Kimba brought a comfort to Asmodeus that he had not felt in many years. He looked to the sparkling stars, certain his brother had something to do with it.

"Thank you, brother," he softly said to the twinkling sky.

Kukulkan grew strangely quiet, bringing about an unexplained calm over Asmodeus. Time became warped as the memory of his recent, intense, power surge floated away. He searched the star-speckled sky for answers as he sat listening to Kimba's rhythmic, deep breathing. Gradually, the combination of the two nudged Asmodeus into the world beyond awareness.

The tall reeds rustled in the gentle morning breeze.

In full panic mode, Gaia flung her dusty body out of the crevice at the bottom of the stairs. She paused to see if she was being pursued, but only the barren stairs remained. Quickly, she fled towards the tall grasses ahead. Fleetingly, she wondered what happened to the young garter she had seen crushed by Mandihar's army, but her brain didn't let her dwell on it, shrieking at her to keep moving. Before diving into safety, Gaia took one last look at Kukulkan. The towering formation stood majestically quiet as it always had for thousands of years. The moon had disappeared as light-grey rain clouds closed in. A light mist began sprinkling from the dreary sky, gently cleansing Kukulkan. Gaia speedily slithered to the river with her only thought being survival, but it wasn't long before utter exhaustion forced her to stop next to the lapping water on the riverbank's stones. As she took a deep breath, she noticed something different. The air was heavier than normal, yet somehow comforting to her tortured soul. Even better, it induced sleep—sweet oblivion.

Then the dream started. Fleeting faces of all those she loved floated in and out of a heavy mist, interspersed with vivid flashes of carnage and death. The mist parted slightly and there was a door, barely cracked, with a bright beam of light shining through. The voices of HOXD and Miss Hissy argued in the background.

"I told you how wrong you are, Gaia!" Miss Hissy shouted.

HOXD calmly answered, repeating a line from his prayer to the universe. "Show us light out of darkness!"

His voice echoed several times in the mist before fading away.

Gaia's parents appeared, calling for her as she moved toward a closed door of strange colors that emitted crackling noises, making it seem alive. She slowly slithered toward it as the voices grew faint, and as she approached the door, it magically opened. A flood of blue light poured out, and a brown tower lurked beyond. Suddenly, a large snake tail curled around Gaia's tail and began pulling her toward her parents; she struggled to get free but couldn't. Ahead of her, the muted background lit up with a pulsating purple light, blinding Gaia temporarily. As the tail pulled her back, the light field emitted a force so strong it pulled her forward. A deafening scream exploded into the air as Gaia's body began to be pulled apart.

Gaia's body writhed in her fitful sleep before she sat straight up in a panic, her heart pounding. Her face was wet from the rain. It was nature's tears—tears Gaia couldn't control. Like the rushing waters of the river, they flowed down her face, and when the river ran dry, the tears turned inward.

Gaia didn't know how long she had been coiled in the weeds just staring over the flowing water. She did know, though, that after what she had learned, she could never really go home again. She also knew she would never abandon those she loved. With a conflicted soul, she slithered onto the path and turned toward Moon Meadow, but without a doubt in her mind, she knew she'd be back.

ABOUT THE AUTHORS

Aniko Brang is a writer and a fan of anything outside the box. She was born in Minnesota and continues to live there with her husband. She is a registered nurse. Aniko believes in being true to yourself and to never stop dreaming.

Nancy Saros is a writer, born in Minnesota and currently residing there. Widowed early, she raised three children by working in the business world, writing as she could. Nancy offers a lifetime of unbridled curiosity, which has taken her into unimagined fields of ancient knowledge and amazing discoveries. Today she writes to keep that curiosity alive, especially in the young.

Printed in the USA
CPSIA information can be obtained
at www.ICGtesting.com
LVHW011641100124
768373LV00003BA/73